Tales of Dorset

Tales of Dorset

OLIVE KNOTT'S COLLECTIVE STORIES

Printed and Published by

THE FRIARY PRESS LTD.

Friary Lane, Dorchester, Dorset

1976

TO THE MEMORY OF MY
FATHER WHO INSPIRED THESE
RUSTIC TALES.

ISBN 0 902043 21 8

FOREWORD

This reprint of my three books, *Down Dorset Way*, *More About Dorset* and *Dorset Again*, first published by the Friary Press 1952, 1954 and 1956 respectively, gives me a great deal of pleasure as the demand for them which has persisted over the years, may now be supplied.

The subject matter is very diverse but all of Dorset flavour. Many of the tales were related by my father in our childhood days. In fact he has always been the inspiration of my Dorset writings.

I am especially pleased that this reprint includes a number of dialect stories and so will be a means of preserving the 'Folk Speech' as William Barnes calls it, which, alas, is fast dying out.

ACKNOWLEDGMENTS

I wish to thank all those who so kindly supplied first-hand information concerning the old days.

ILLUSTRATIONS

by

K. L. G. HART

COVER PHOTOGRAPH

This delightful rural picture taken by the late Mr. C. R. Stride at Fiddleford in 1951, comes from Mr. Raymond Rogers' collection of old Sturminster photographs.

The driver of the wagon is Mr. Fred Yeatman, for fifty years carter to the Rose family at the Fiddleford Mill, and the small boy nestled against him is Sydney, aged three, son of Mr. Rupert Rose, the present miller and farmer at Fiddleford Mill.

The Rose family have held the mill since 1874 and 'Worthy Bloom the Miller' of whom William Barnes wrote so amusingly, is none other than the great grandfather of Mr. Rupert Rose and incidentally the great, great, grandfather of the boy in the wagon.

CONTENTS

Shroton Fair 9
Wold John 12
How Silas was Prevented 14
The Dogs Do Bark 17
Garge's Valentine 23
April Vools 25
Lament for Poole Fair 27
An Old Dorset Yuletide 28
Dorset 31
Poole 32
Poole Fair 33
A Tree 34
Poole—Down on the Quay 35
The Dorsetshire Lake District 36
The Village of Hammoon 38
Spring Ramble to Chapman's Pool 41
Autumn Ramble to Woolsbarrow 43
The Great Frost of 1890 44
Old Dorset Superstitions 45
The Club Walk 47
Christmas in Old Poole 51
Rustic Transport 53
Bird Starvin 56
The Unloved Society 58
The Good Old Days of Methodism 59
Lizer Ann 61
A Shot in the Dark 64
The Countryman Scores 65

ANCESTRAL

The Village of Hinton St. Mary 68
The Old Rectory, Hamworthy 72
Plumber Manor 75
Racedown 79
Kingston Lacey 83
Woolbridge Manor 87

RURAL

Sturminster Newton in the Old Days 91
Dorset Superstitions 98
Woodbury Hill and its Fair 101

CONTENTS

Among the Dorset Gypsies 105
The Gipsy's Funeral 111
The Reddle Woman 115

RUSTIC

All round Archit 118
Varmer Brickell and the Ghost 122
The Wrong Man 125
A Dosset Man in London 127
Ground up a-vresh 129
Washington's Own Honour 131
POEM: The Mossy Bridge Athirt the Stream 137

PERSONALITIES

A Dorset Granny 138
The Veteran Artist of Studland 141
The Martyrs of Tolpuddle 145
Orme Angus, the Inspired School-Master 149
Granny Cousins, the last of the Knockers-up in Poole .. 153
Billy, the Parrot of Honeymead Lane 156
POEM: Waitin' for Jenny 159

PLACES

Stinsford 160
Brownsea Island 163
Wareham 168
The Village of Horton 171
Spetisbury 175
Bere Regis 178
POEM: Late Spring 182

SOME DORSET INNS

The Square and Compass 184
The Blacksmith's Arms 187
The King's Stag Inn 189
The Damory Oak 191
The Bull's Head 194
World's End 197

Miss Billetts Fortune 201
The Lavender Lady 205

SHROTON FAIR

A WEST COUNTRY MONOLOGUE

"Ah ! I always liked t' go t' Shroton Fair, but there were oone occasion I shall never forgit, and that were the time when I took the prettiest maid in the village in my wold dunkey-cart. I were a smartish lad in they days wi' me collar and tie and the maidens did look saucy at me, but I 'ad eyes for none o' 'em but pretty Fanny Day.

Me heart gi' a thud as I helped 'er up an' she sat beside me, for she looked a picture in 'er flowery cotton gown, 'er comely face a-smilin'. She did chat as we jogged along and the dunkey did goo as I'd never known'n goo afore. Then I can mind how I begun t' zing. I used t' do a bit a-zingin' in they days, but wi' she beside me in thik wold dunkey-cart I wouldn't a-changed places wi' the King on his throne ! Zoo we did jog along. Jiggity-jig ; Jiggerty-jig ! an' other volks did pass us a-gwine t' Shroton Fair. By and by we come to the bottom o' Hambledon Hill and from there we could zee the Huntsmen a-gettin' ready t' be off. They did always meet there afore the fair. They were a pretty sight, the red and black coats showed up agin the green o' the hillside, but my sonnies, when they were hard-slig-gallop down the hill it fair took yer breath away.

Fanny, she clapped her hands an' zaid, " Oh, Ambrose, look at them jumping hedges and ditches ! "

" But it's a cruel sport," she zaid. She were a tender-hearted maid ; leastways, she were over animals.

Well, then we went on to the fair-field.

" What shall us do fust ? " I zaid. " There's round-a abouts, swings, shootin' galleries, cocoa-nut shies, switch-backs, hooplas, fortune tellers, conjurers ! " She laughed, and I never 'eard a maid laugh like Fanny, so merry like.

" We'll go on the round-abouts ? " she said, and zoo we did. The music did blare out, and up and down an' round an' round we went ; my hoss were close beside 'ers and when she were up, I were down. Then I most wished I'd a-bed on the ground, so that I could've a-volleyed 'er round wi' me eye. Ah ! I thought t' mezelf, before Shroton Fair be over I be a-gwine t' ax she t' be my wife.

But when we were down agen and strollin' about, I didn't know how t' make a start. There were t' much of a hub-bub for oone thing and I should a'had to a'shouted for everyone d'hear so I put it off. I put it off, I zay agen, an' let this be a warnin' t' all you young fellers, a maid be never in the zame mind twice, so pop the question quick, if you've a-mind to marry and don't bide beatin' about the bush. If I'd a-asked 'er then, maybe things 'ud a-ben different, but then—I've a-lived ever since wi'out a wooman, an' zeen many a man make a wuss fool o' hisself !

I got s' far as " Fanny, Fanny," an' I could veel me neck hot under my collar, when she put 'er hand on my arm an' called out, " There's Aunt Caroline and Uncle Dick ! " And sure enough, there they were, a-standin' behind their stall a-sellin' pastries and cakes and brandy-balls. So we 'ad t'ave a word wi' they and she did laugh and 'er Uncle Dick did chuck 'er under th' chin while I stood up like a girt dummy wishin' I could do the zame. She didn't zeem t' mind neither, so I thought t' meself, "Ambrose, what's the good t' be shy. Why 'er old Uncle Dick be spryer then you ! Well, then we went round t' the cocoa-nut shies, and I paid out my spite on they. I knocked down dree straight off, an' that's what I wanted t' do wi' all they fellers a-makin' sheep's eyes at my Fanny. We 'ad a goo at the hooplas, chuckin' rings, y'know, and I'm hanged if between us we didn' win a clock and a couple of vases. Luck in everything but love, I thought t' meself. Well, the time wore on, an' still I 'adn' declared meself. You could a-counted up on your two hands the number o' words I zaid to 'er all day. I kep thinkin' to meself, she wouldn' a-come wi' you, Ambrose my son, in your dunkey-cart if she 'adn' bin partial t' 'ee. She wouldn't chat and laugh wi' you wi' other fellers round if it weren't you she chose. Ah ! but

I didn't know wimmin, and I didn't understand their ways then, as I do now.

Ambrose, my son, I thought, when you be jog-trottin' whome, an it's all peaceful a'n quiet, she'll be tired an' you can just slip yer arm round 'er waist, an' p'raps . . . . . well, the next move'll depend on how she d'take that. Zoo, all at once I were terrible anxious to be gettin' whome along, but Fanny, she be minded t' stay. Then it begun t' git dusk, and the volks were thinnin' down, so she turned to I an' zaid, "Ambrose, let's go home." Quick as lightnin' I hitched in the dunkey, 'elped 'er up beside me, an' off we went. Now, Ambrose, I zaid to meself, pop the question quick, avore she got time to zimmer down. " Shroton Fair 'ave come and Shroton Fair 'ave gone," I begun. She looked round at I, 'er eyes a-dancin'. " I've won dree coco-nuts, a clock, a couple o' vases, but," I zaid, an' I could veel me 'eart gi' a thud, " There were zummit else I wanted to win ! " "Ambrose, don't be greedy," she said. Then thinkin' p'raps she didn't know what I meant, I slipped me arm round 'er waist, an' were jist a-gwine t' make it plain when the cart gi' a lurch and we were both pitched out on the green beside o' the road. We both sat up an' looked at each other, but narn o' us were hurt. Then she pointed to the dunkey and laughed like she always did. There were my pore wold dunkey sound asleep in the middle o' the road. " Never mind, Ambrose," she said, " I've won my bet."

" Won your bet ? " I zaid.

" Yes, someone laid a wager with me that I wouldn't ride to Shroton Fair in a donkey cart ! "

So I never axed 'er after all ! I whipped up the dunkey and kep' 'un awake till we got whome. Then I 'anded 'er down, and I made a vow in me 'eart that I 'ud fight shy o' wimmin, especially the comely oones, an' turn me attention t' hosses and dunkeys.

A good many Shroton Fairs 'ave come an' gone since then, an' a good many pretty wenches have looked my way ; but niver since then 'ave I axed a maid, be she comely or not, t' ride wi' I in my wold dunkey cart.

An' many a feller 'ave come t' I t' complain o' the way their wives d' treat 'em, but I d'zay, " You axed 'er diden't 'ee ? "

'Twere my wold dunkey that stopped I, or I should ha' bin in the zame boat meself ! "

WOLD JOHN

A TALE OF CONSTANT LOVE

We all knew that wold John's wife was dead. She had been gone this forty year and he hadn't got chick nor child belongin' to'n.

But every night we zeed, and there was no mistakin', mind you, his wife a-zittin' at the head o' his table.

Wold John never drawed down his blind ; maybe he never had one, for he were a-past work except for a few odd jobs now and again. We often wondered how he kept body and soul together.

No, there was never no blind in his window and when he'd got his little lamp a-lit we could zee 'er as plain as a pike-staff.

We wold chaps could mind when she first a-come to the village and a pretty bit o' goods she was. Her hair were golden like the colour o' carn when 'tis ripe an' she had a way we' 'er which pretty nigh mazed poor wold John. Well, he were young John then an' sprightly enough as far as young fellers d' go.

So he wed 'er down at the little Church and seein' as how they lived so happy, the pair o' 'em always attended Church regular and if ever we zid 'em about they were always arm in arm.

Ay, she were a pretty bit o' goods, an' John told me once wi' his own lips that many's the time he've a-struck a light in the middle o' the night to see her golden hair bezide 'n on the pillow.

" Yes," I zaid, "your wife is the best lookin' woman in this place. There's narn t' hold a candle to 'er unless," I zaid, " 'tis the hairdresser's model in the barber's shop window, and they be alike as two peas."

" That may be," he zaid, " but she is but wax and my Mary is flesh an' blood."

Well, time went on an' I should think they had been married about a twelve-month when his wife were a-taken ill. John were up night and day, the doctor were a-called in, but it were no good ; she died and they laid 'er down there in the little churchyard and John were left alone.

From that time on he turned queer an' had nothing to do with nobody year in, year out. We used t' zee'n about but never once did anyone see'n down churchyard. " 'Tis mighty funny," we said, "zeein' as how he were so fond o' 'er."

The grass growed long over her grave and never a flower did he put there.

Well, as I've said avore, at night time we could zee wi' our own eyes his wife a-zittin' at the head o' his table dressed in her pretty blue gown that she'd a-worn to church an' up an' down the country lanes o' Sundays.

We zid her golden hair the same as ever, a-piled up on her head and there were John a-noddin' an' a-talkin' to 'er as he did in her life-time.

Now I'm not what you mid call a superstitious man, but zeein' is believin', and there avore our very eyes were John's wife, Mary, who had been dead this forty year.

For, in case my eyes deceived me, I called together a few more chaps an' we watched his window o' nights, and every night regular we saw the same thing, wold John's wife a-zittin' at his table.

The years went by an' all the village now believed that wold John's wife had a-come back from the dead to keep'n company o' nights.

So we left'n alone an' he seemed t' be happy enough. He never talked to his neighbours although we could hear'n a-talkin' to '*er* plain enough.

Well, there come one dark winter evening when wold John forgot to light his lamp and the little cottage was all in darkness.

We missed the light from his window as his house was a-top o' the hill an' you could see the glow a mile away.

Next day I zaid, " There's summit wrong wi' wold John. He've never a-missed to light up his lamp o' winter nights this forty year. I'm a-goin' t' zee."

So I went up the hill to his tumble-down cottage and walked straight in. There I zid the table a-laid for two all set out as neat and tidy as you please, but no sign of any living creature.

Then I went upstairs to his bedroom and what I saw there I shall never forget to me dying day.

For there in bed lay poor wold John wi' a smile on his face an' I didn't need t' look twice t' zee that he were dead, and beside'n wi' her golden hair all over the pillow were not Mary, his wife, but the waxen image from the barber's shop all dressed up in a white nightgown.

They lay there together for all the world as if 'twas their weddin' night'

" Poor wold John, you be where she is now for sure," I zaid, and covered 'em over wi' the sheet.

HOW SILAS WAS PREVENTED

Volks 'ave always ben curious t' know why I bain't married, zoo if you be minded t' listen I'll tell 'ee the reason why.

Fust of all, I 'ould like 'ee t' know that my wold mother were a good 'ooman. She'd a-read the Bible from cover t' cover, an' tha's more'n can be zaid o' zome o' em. Bit she 'ad what you mid call a bee in 'er bonnet. She didn' want fer I t' marry. Mid-be 'twere on account o' my wold father a-treatin' o' 'er s' bad.

He left 'er when I were two year old t' work 'er vingers t' the bone t' bring I up respectable.

Zoo, in consequence o' it, any maid that I did vancy, she did vind fault wi' an' try t' zet I agin 'er.

There were oone I were terrible vond o', fer she were a purty liddle maid. " Don't thee 'ave she," me mother zaid, "she don't like work. She'll bring thee t' the work'ouse wi' 'er lazy ways."

Zoo, I gid 'er up. Then I can 'mind another I ad, tall, she were, 'an' thin.

" If you d' marry she," me mother zaid, "she'll run be'ind 'ee wi' the dust-pan brush an' make 'ee take thee boots off outside thee own door."

Zoo, I gid she up, too.

Well, then I vound another, an' this time I made up me mind that whativer me mother did zay, I were agwaine t' marry she.

Zoo, I zettles down t' courtin' reglar. " Don'ee marry thick thin-lipped wench," me mother cried out, "thee 'oon't be maister in thee own 'ouse. Why she've got a temper like a viper, an' a tongue like a whip. Wha's more she'll starve thee, I tell 'ee, she'll starve thee. She'd put 'er 'and in hell, fer a ha'penny ! She's wuss than t' other two.

But I turned a deaf ear and proceeded wi' me courtship. Twice a wik we did meet, Wednesdays an' Zundays. On Wednesdays, I can mind, I used t' put on me zecond best, but on Zundays I did put on bestest, an' then we did meet at the liddle wicket-geate leadin' int' the copse, at dree o'clock.

Now my wold mother knowed exactly when an' where we did meet, fer what she couldn' zee, she did vind out.

Oone particlar Zunday adernoon I dressed meself very careful an' looked a bit longer in the glass mid-be. Any'ow I could sware me mother knowed that I'd a-made up me mind t' pop the question fer she looked at I wi' a meanin' look as much as t'zay " You poor vool, you oon't be told."

Howiver, she didn' zay nothin' bit come t' door when I went on, wi' a vunny smile on 'er face, an waved 'er 'and as I went out o' the geate.

It were apple-pickin' time I can mind, but still warm an' mellow.

She'll be wearin' thick blue silk dress, I thought t' meself, an' thick liddle bonnet decked up wi' vlowers.

I'll ax 'er to-day, an' mid-be be Christmas we can be wed.

Now I d' zometimes think that a man's life is sart a planned out for'n. Anyway, there was zummit or zomebody who said " No, Silas, my son, you cain't 'ave 'er," fer avore I got t' the liddle wicket geate I zeed 'er astandin' there in 'er blue silk gown and bonnet decked up wi' vlowers.,

But, she were not be 'erself, fer there bezide 'er were Nat Harper, me rival in love. They was standin' close togither an' as I got nearer I could zee that Nellie's cheeks were rid an' 'er eyes a-flashin'.

" Wha's the meanin' o' this ? " I zays, comin' up close to 'em.

" The meanin' o' it is " zays Nellie, "you've a-kep I waitin' yer a whole half-hour." I should ha' ben gone bit I've a-stayed t' tell 'ee what I think o' 'ee. A lazy good-fer-nothin' tha's what you be ! Idden he, Nat ? "

"Ay, he is," zays Nat, an' he 'ad a grin on 'is face that did very nearly drive I mad.

" Mid-be you'd let I 'ave a word ? " I zaid, " Fer one thing, I bain't a half-hour late, 'tis dree o'clock t' the minute," an' I whips me watch out o' me pocket t' testify t' the truth o' it. Then I felt me jaw drop, fer sure enough 'twere hafe-past-dree.

" There's a mistake somewhere," I zaid.

" Oh yes, there's a mistake all right," says Nellie, high and mighty. " The mistake you made Silas Day is t' come a-courtin' I."

" You need'n come no more " an' she tossed 'er 'ead, crooked 'er arm in Nat's an' off they went togither drew the woods.

" Well, that d' beat all " I zaid t' meself. I cain't under-stand it. Our wold clock at home were right this marnin'. Niver knowed'n lose time avore.

But fancy she takin' on like that there all on account o' a hafe-hour's waitin'.

" There, 'tis noo good upzettin' yerself, Silas, my zon" I zays, wipin' a tear from me eye. 'Twadden t' be ! 'Twad-den t' be ! Me wold mother an' Providence be o' the zame mind.

Well, I niver breathed no word t' me mother about what 'ad 'appened. She axed me, I can mind, why I were back s' soon.

" Oh," I zaid, an' I 'low God forgi'e me fer the lie, " I just popped out t' post a letter."

Well, the time passed by an' the next thing I heard were that Nat an' Nellie were married.

I kep' me eye on 'em, an' as the years went by I zid me mother's words a-comin' true.

Nat, he did git thinner an' thinner, he did slouch along wi' 'is 'ead down an' anybody could zee wi' only hafe a eye that a-were the most hen-pecked man in the village.

"A tyrant she be," he whispered t' zomebody, " I be hafe-starved an' I be aveard t' spake out me own mind."

Then there come the day when me poor wold mother died.

" Silas," she said, " I've a-got a confession t' make to 'ee."

" What can it be ? " I zaid, " You niver done I no harm."

" No, I didn' harm thee, Silas," she zaid, " but I must tell 'ee the truth avore I d' go."

" Do 'ee mind that Sunday afternoon a long while back, when you was late t' meet thick maid ? "

" Ah, I mind," I answered.

" Well," she zaid, " I put the clock back hafe-an-hour, a purpose t' make 'ee late." " I knowed she were a spit-vire."

" Don't thee worry about that there, mother," I zaid, " When I zees what Nat Harper 'ave a-come to, I be turrible glad thee did."

" Don't-thee-niver-marry-Silas," she said, then she vell back an' died.

THE DOGS DO BARK

A TALE OF AN OLD MARKET TOWN

The story is related by " Wold Garge " in an old tavern in the town of Stour Cross.

" Garge " is the village philosopher who sits back and takes notice.

Volks d' zometimes zay that this is a sleepy wold place an' nothin' do ever happen but I d' zay that if things don't happen now they used t' do.

Why, this yer place was teemin' wi' happenin's. Murderers have a-gone unhung in this liddle town, gone to their grave an' had a decent burial when they should have a-swung on the gallows. Perfect crimes was done that have never ben brought t' light, exceptin' when 'twas too late for justice t' be done.

Well, now I'm goin' t' tell 'ee a tale me wold gran'fer used t' tell altho' he never lived t' zee the end o' it.

'Twas a long time ago, mid-be s' much as a hundred year, when a respectable doctor 'ad 'is surgery in the Market Place. They called 'n Doctor Jack. He lived wi' 'is wife in a fine house in the best part o' the town.

Flourishin' he was, for he had what we should call t-day a bed-side manner an' the wimmen volk wi' a bit o' money were always a-callin' o'n in. There were oone lady in particlar he were for iver dancin' attendance on. She pretty well kep'n goin'. She did call'n in fer a cold in the head or a vinger ache an' he did run up bills, 'twas said, enough t' frighten 'ee, but she didn't zeem t' mind. There were noo doubt about it she were thoroughly took up wi' 'n.

This yer doctor never missed Church of a Sunday marnin' an' neither did this ailin' 'ooman. Often when they were a-zingin' o' the psalms she d' vall over in a swoon an' the doctor did carry 'er out. Some volks said she done it a-purpose.

For, mind you, the doctor were a good-lookin' man. He 'ad dark curly hair, an' blue eyes (Irish I shouldn' wonder), bit he 'ad a tiddy liddle mouth, that didn' seem right fer a man. However, the women-volk did'n mind that. They thought the world o'n. But some o' the poor volks did say that the toffs did pay'n fer 'is smiles an' 'is bows an' that they 'ad more money than sense.

Now, 'twere a funny thing, mark you, that though the women-volk were s' took up wi' 'n all the dogs in the place did hate the sight o' 'n. They did snarl an' growl when they sid'n comin', an' many's the time when he went to somebody's door he'd have t'call out " Madam, will you please call yer dog off ! " avore he could step inside.

There were oone occasion I heard tell o' when a woman were martal bad an' doctor Jack were sent for, but when he got t' house 'er dog 'ud'n let'n goo in an' the poor soul died. She could ha' ben saved, mind 'ee, if s' be the doctor could 'ave attended 'er.

As I said avore, doctor Jack were doin' well in these liddle town o' Stour Cross. Altho' when he fust come t' the place he had'n a-got a ha'penny t' bless hiself wi', he made 'is money wi' his good looks an' plausible ways—and mind you, he were clever. Oh yes, he knowed just what t' do, no matter what volks 'ad the matter wi' 'em—an' what he didn' know about the workin's o' peoples' insides wad'n worth knowin'.

Then a-married money too. He had'n a-ben yer long avore he made up t' the lawyer's woldest daughter. I reckon he knowed what he were about fer 'er father were rollin' in money. She wurden much t' look at, but a real lady if ever there were oone.

All the town thought that doctor Jack had done well fer hiself an' his marriage did certainly zet'n on his feet.

You can understand then, that doctor Jack were a wealthy man when things begun t' happen to'n.

Oone day in November, about four o'clock in the adernoon, I were told, when Stour Cross were all peaceful an' quiet, a woman come t' the place 'oldin' a child b' the hand.

Now, if s' be it had a-ben a market day, mid-be volks wouldn' have a-took much notice o'em but the place were very near empty at the time so the news soon got about that strangers had a-come t' town. The shop-keepers come t' their doors t' have a look an' a word wi' 'em if they could.

The woman was round about thirty years old an' though she 'ad a hard look (exceptin' when she did look at the child) you could see that she had a-ben very good lookin' She was dressed very poor an' both she an' the liddle maid looked as though they could do wi' a good square meal.

Now, as I d' say far, the volks did stare at 'em, but 'twas mostly at the liddle maid they did bide an' stare for she were a reglar beauty.

'Twas true 'er cheeks were pinched an' 'er clothes were ragged an' dirty but she had beautiful dark curly hair, an' 'er eyes were s' blue as carn flowers.

She did cling to 'er mother's hand an' the pair o' 'em did look as forlorn a couple as ever you'd zee in a day's march.

Now volks soon found out that they'd a-come down from Hilltown workhouse, tramped all the way on foot. Then they got out o' the woman that she were looking' fer somebody. At vust she wouldn' tell who she'd a-come t' vind, but at last they got it out o' 'er that she were a-lookin' fer a doctor who 'ad once ben at Maidenborough at the same time as she'd a-lived there in service. She were respectable then, she zaid.

His name, she told 'em, was—well, I oon't say his name because mid-be some o' his descendants be still alive.

Oh, they said, you d' mean Doctor Jack! Oh, ah, he d' live yer, sure enough, but wha's the madder wi' you that you've a-come all this way d' zee he?

Then the woman zaid "There's nought the matter wi' I exceptin' me heart's a-cold an' me belly's empty."

Well, they zaid to 'er, doctors don't usually zet up their surgerys t' warm women-volks' hearts nor t' vill their bellies.

"No," she said, "I'm not expectin' he'll ever warm me heart any more but mid-be he'll help me for the sake o' the child."

"Well, there's noo harm in tryin', missus," they zaid, "but Doctor Jack's the wrong man t' throw 'is money about."

Then they looked at the liddle maid an' back again at the mother an' zaid nothin' at all, but they thought the more I d' low for anybody could zee wi' on'y hafe a eye that the liddle oone were the very daps o' doctor Jack.

She were bent on seein' o'n, so the volks told 'er t' goo along b' the Town cross an' close along side o'n she'd see the doctor's surgery. "You'll be sure d' vind'n there," they zaid, "for he d' spend hours a-mixin' up 'is medicines." "Sometimes," they told 'er, he d' bide there t' midnight pokin' about. Whatever 'is wife d' think o' it we don' know."

Be now all the town had a-got t'know about the woman, an' the liddle maid. They put their 'eads together an' whispered t' each other. 'Twere on'y the same wold story over again but because 'twere Doctor Jack it zet the town agog.

" He'll turn 'er away," some said. " No he oon't," t' others whispered, " He'll gie 'er some money t' keep 'er quiet. He got enough o' it."

Then some did say that when he did see the child, s' like hiself, his 'eart 'ud be touched an' he'd git his wife to adopt 'er.

Zoo all the town were watchin' when the two o' 'em went to the surgery door. They peeped from their winders an' door-ways or made it their business t' be walkin' casual by the place.

Then as they were a long time a-comin' out again volks zaid " He must be attendin' to 'em or they would have a-come out quicker."

Now, a very funny thing happened that night, an' if I didn't know 'twere gospel-true I wouldn' a-believed it.

'Twas about eleven o'clock when somebody's dog zet up a-howlin', very pitiful. Then another started in answer to he, an' presently all the dogs in the town were a-howlin' together.

I shouldn' think anybody in the town 'ad a wink o' sleep thick night. 'Twere all s' quiet apart from the dogs, that nobody could make it out.

Heads popped out o' winders and zome I were told, even got up out o' their beds and went t' door t' 'ave a look out but they couldn' zee nothin' at all different from usual. There wadden a soul about an' there was the light in the window o' doctor Jack's surgery same as it always were—but there were a feelin'—a creepy strange feelin', an' I reckon they dogs could veel it too.

'Twere town's talk next marnin'. " Whativer were the matter wi' all the dogs ? " they zaid t' one another. But nobody knowed. Then all the town did wish that dogs could talk for they guessed they knowed zummit that human bein's didn'.

Well, as time went on volks begun t' forgit about the howlin' o' the dogs an' nobody made enquiries about the woman an' the child since everybody thought they'd a-gone on t' the next workhouse. " Poor things," they zaid, " 'tis t' be hoped the doctor took pity on 'em.

Nobody had the neck t' mention 'em to doctor Jack but then he didn' give 'em the chance an' then the next thing they heard about 'n was that he'd a-gone away an' zet up practice in London.

" That were quick work," volks zaid, "whatever made he leave the place s' sudden ? " " I 'low," zome o' 'em zaid, " He couldn't put up wi' the dogs a-snarlin' an' a-growlin' at 'n."

Ver true enough, they wouldn' let'n goo into volks' houses an' oone day a liddle black terrier got 'old of his leg an' bit 'n through 'is trousers.

Zoo doctor Jack left the town wi' his wife an' liddle bwoy an' a new doctor come in 'is place.

He had 'is surgery at 'is house, zoo they decided to do up the place where doctor Jack 'ad 'is, an' make it into a dwellin'.

It looked smart enough when 'twere done an' 'twas soon took b' some people who 'ad a beautiful black retriever. They thought gold o' this yer dog an' used t' have 'n indoor wi' 'em night and day, but the dog wouldn' goo inside this 'ouse. They coaxed 'n an' done everything they could t' tole 'n in but he wouldn' cross the threshold.

Zoo the volks wouldn' goo in neither. " There's zummit about thick house," they zaid, " mid-be 'tis haunted," an' they vound another place.

Then rumours begun t' git about that a light was zid t' come up in the middle o' the night an' shadows on the blind. 'Twas a woman, they zaid, you could zee it as plain as a pikestaff, a woman wi' a child a-clinging to 'er skirts.

Zoo nobody 'ud take the house where doctor Jack's surgery had a-ben, an' the place bed empty fer years.

Zome long time after—when volks 'ad most forgot about the doctor the women-volk liked an' the dogs couldn' abide, zomebody got hold o' a London paper, an' the news of what was in 'n spread all over the town. " Death an' funeral of well-known an' famous physician," it zaid. It give 'is full name (which I oon't repeat) an' zaid that in 'is younger days he had a practice in the West Country in the small market town o' Stour Cross.

He 'ad a big funeral, it zaid, an' he were vollered to 'is grave b' the Lord Mayor an' other important City volk.

There were noo doubt about it, 'twere, doctor Jack, buried wi' pomp an' circumstance.

Then volks who could mind about the woman an' the child that come t' see 'n, zaid they couldn' 'ave a-spoiled 'is chances ader all.

Years went by an' still nobody 'ud live in the house where the surgery 'ad a-ben, zoo 'twere decided at last t' make 'n into offices. "If volks oon't live in 'n," they zaid "mid-be they'll work in 'n." S' many years 'ad a-gone by, that the boards were a-rottin' so the fust thing they 'ad t' do were t' take up the floor.

Now what I be a-goin' t' tell 'ee be Gospel-true, fer I zid it wi' me own eyes. Bein' a carpenter be trade as you do all know, I helped t' take up the floor so that new boards could be laid, an' in consequence o' it I were the vust oone t' zet eyes upon what was hid beneath.

Then I knowed what they dogs knowed s' long ago, about the man who'd a-gone to 'is grave wi' such pomp an' ceremony.

For underneath they rottin' boards I saw two skeletons.

Oone mid-have ben a woman but for certain, t' other were a child.

GARGE'S VALENTINE

I were always terrible shy when I were young. None o' the lads in the village were half s' shy as I.

It didn't matter if a maid were plain, I could, mid-be, speak a word or two to 'er, but if she were comely an' nice t' look upon, why, then I were all a-blushin' an' a-stammerin'.

It wouldn't of a-mattered much if there hadn't a-ben oone maid I longed t' talk to, but there were, an' I couldn' s' much as say " Good day " to 'er.

Why God-a-mighty made me s' shy I can't tell, but it were St. Valentine who helped me out o' it. 'Twere fifty year ago now, but I shall niver forget that day an' the consequences o' it.

I can mind the day avore I'd a-ben out ploughin'. " The rooks be nestin'," I thought t' meself, " the song-birds be a-chirpin' an' the leaves be comin' on the trees."

Then I dreamed as the plough went up an' down the vield, of a cosy nest wi' *'er*.

" But Garge," I said t' meself, " that'll never be, if you cain't a-speak yer mind to 'er."

Well then, as I were on my way home, I passed the little watch-maker's shop, an' zid a' were all decked up wi' Valentines. Some o' 'em were a yard long wi' ugly drawin's on 'em an' verses t' suit 'em. Then me eye vell upon a little dainty one, w' flowers all round 'n and dree words across the middle ; dree words I'd a-ben longin' t' zay to 'er for close on eighteen months. I felt meself goo hot, but pluckin' up me courage I went in the shop an' bought 'n. Then out I come and straight home, put 'n in an envelope an' posted 'n to 'er avore I could change me mind. I heard 'n drop in the letter box.

" Well done, Garge," I zaid t' meself. " You've a-zaid it at last."

That night, as I were a-bed, I thought to meself, " You fool, Garge, you ought to 'ave put yer name to'n. She'll never know who sent 'n."

However, next mornin' there was a big rat-tat at the door, an' bein' an early riser, I answered 'n meself. 'Twas the postman wi' zummit for me.

I opened it an' there avore my eyes were the very same Valentine, an' they dree words a-starin' up at me. Then somethin' told me it were *she*.

" I love 'er an' she d' love me," I thought.

Me heart was thuddin', an' I were blushin' as I went down the road.

" What's the matter, Garge, had a fortune left 'ee ? " my mate zaid as I passed 'n.

" Ah, dropped in the letter-box," I zaid.

Then comin' up the road who should I zee but Jenny, my maid I'd a-thought on for so long.

" You be my Valentine, Jenny," I zaid, forgettin' I was shy. " Be I yourn ? "

" Yes, Garge," she answered, " you be."

APRIL VOOLS

I shall niver forgit the time when my wold 'ooman made a vool o' me.

I'd noticed several days avore April Vool Day that she did bide lookin' at me wi' a double-cunnin' look, as much as t' zay " I got 'ee this time." I didn't take much notice o' it at the time, although I did think to meself now and again, " What's up wi' mother ? ", but I niver once thought she'd a-caught me. For up to now, mark you, I could catch mother as easy as winkin', but niver *once* could she catch I.

I can mind one marnin' on the vust of April sayin' to 'er quite casual-like as we sat eatin' our breakfast, " Mother, there's zummit crawlin' up your back ! "

Up she jumped, screechin' and callin' out, " Take it off, Garge, take it off."

" Oh, you April Vool," I said.

Then another time I zaid to 'er, "Mother, fancy zittin down t' table wi' a face like that ! Why, you've a-got a girt smear all across 'n."

Then up she jumped, ran to the lookin' glass, and peered in.

" What you can zee in the glass, mother," I zaid, "is a *girt big April Vool.*"

" Oh, Garge," she zaid, "you be too smart for me. You made a vool o' me when you fust took me t' church, an' you've a-kept it up iver since."

Well, all this was avore the day that mother made a vool o' me, but now when April Vool Day d' come along, I d' bide quiet.

Avore I tell 'ee how it happened, I must zay that ivery marnin' at half-a-past six, I d' git up, make a cup o' tay and take one up t' mother. Then I d' go down an' light the vire while mother's a-gettin' up.

On this particular vust of April, I woke up early, full o' little ideas of how t' catch mother again. I zid the clock pointed t' half a-past six. So I jumped out o' bed and dressed as quick as I could. I can mind I thought how cold and dark it seemed for the time o' year, but attached no importance to it then.

I crope downstairs, put on the kettle, made a cup o' tea and brought 'n up to mother.

" Wake up, mother," I zaid, " yer's yer tea."

She took a lot o' wakin' but at last she opened 'er eyes, and then I sid again that double-cunnin' look, but she zaid nothin' at all, jest took 'er tea and sipped it.

Well, then I started on wi' me ealy marnin' duties. I soon had the vire a-cracklin' in the grate.

" Postman's late this marnin'," I thought t' meself, "and how is it I han't heard Ted goo down, an' all the rest o' 'em I d' yer ivery marnin' reg'lar as clock-work ? An' mother, why idden she a-stirrin' ? "

I went t' door an' looked out. Not a soul could I zee.

" Why bless my soul," I zaid, " I be the only oone about !"

" Mother," I called up the stairs, " be you gettin' up ? " But there was no answer.

" Mother," I called again, " git up, 'tis seven a-clock."

Still there was no answer, so I run upstairs and shook 'er hard. Then she sat up in bed an' laughed till I thought she were niver a-goin' t' stop.

" Oh, Garge," she zaid, " you girt April Vool. 'Tis only half a-past vive. I put the clocks on last night after your were a-bed."

LAMENT FOR POOLE FAIR

Poole Vair ain't what it were in my young days. We used t' zave up an' goo in for it hearty, now volks don't zim t' care whether they d' goo or bide whome.

I went round t' other night, an' I thought t' meself, thik amplifier on the round-abouts don't half come up t' th' wold argan! He used t' het up all the latest tuins, an' the music did blare out zoo's you could hear 'n fer miles. Now, upon me Sam, if I 'aint a-got t' put me hand up t' me yer t' ketch the tuin. Thik wold argan used t' play the zame tuin farty times over, but what did we care s' long as 'twas hearty.

An' where's the mud an' slush? I thought t' meself; don't zim like Poole Vair when a veller don't git stuck in the mud.

The booths be pretty much the zame, I thought, but volks don't jine in zame's they used t' do. Ah! that were th' time when Joe Beckett showed 'is vists, an' 'ad 'alf Poole out yer t' watch 'n. None o' yer 'alf 'earted crowd in they days; all a-ready an' up fer a lark!

I can mind when the maidens were as sacy as you like an' the bwoys did chuck confetti over 'em. The prettiest wenches did always git the most, they a-makin' out th' didn't like it, an' all th' time we knowed very well th' did.

An' the zwitch-backs! Where be they? The vun we used t' have a-ridin' up an' down on 'em. We used t' goo up on 'em in a bunch wi' a penny bag of confetti tucked in our waistkit pockets. Then, when the maidens weren't a-lookin' we used t' shoot it over 'em. My! there were a-gigglin' an' a-screamin'.

Aye! Poole Vair ain't what it used t' be! Volks d' all want warmin' up. Truth o' it is, there's t' many things bezide. When volks can goo any night o' th' wik t' the pictures they baint minded t' zave up fer the vair. Ha! I'd zooner shoot down cokernuts and ride on they giddy-hosses wi' a bag o' confetti in me pocket, than I'd zee all the lovely-dovey pictures in creation.

AN OLD DORSET YULE-TIDE

" Come on, father, pile on the logs. 'Tis Christmas Eve ! "

" Ah ! zoo 'tis, mother, an' cold enough t' freeze a brass monkey. Move up the zettle, and Johnny, come closer, you'm lookin' pinched."

Bartholomew Trent surveyed his family gathered around the blazing fire with tolerable contentment. They were all sound in "wind and limb " as far as he knew, unless it was Johnny there, who never seemed as hearty as the rest.

" They b'aint workshy," he often said of them, and indeed they weren't for, at the adjoining farm, of which their small cottage was part, they worked with a will.

" Polly, take down the billis an' puff up the vire a bit. That's more like it. Now that's what I d' *call* a Christmas vire. The flames be roarin' up chimney like sixty ! Goin' t' church they be."

" Bess an' Nellie, you be lookin' pert tonight. Bless my soul if you b'aint a-growin' up, an' more like yer mother every day."

" You've made a proper good do o' the trimmin' up, Bess. Ah, you sly maid, you'm zitting right under the mistletoe. Who do'ee think's a-comin' in ? There's somebody you've a-got up yer sleeve, I d' know ! "

" Where's Sid, father ? " piped Johnny.

" Gone out rantin' up an' down street wi' a whole crowd o' 'em a-singin' their rowdy songs. 'Tis a wonder the policeman han't a-stopped 'em by now. But there, being Christmas Eve, he d' wink his eye at 'em, I 'low."

" Ah, here he is ! Come on, Sid. You be just in time. Mother's about t' dish up the furmity, b'aint you, mother ? That's right, git out the basins an' it's furmity we'll have. Smell good, an' taste better, I d' say."

" That's it. Goo into Johnny ! Don't be a-veard. 'Tis Christmas Eve."

" I cain't eat any more, father."

" Well the, gi' it t' Zid. He'll finish it up."

" There, I knowed he would," as the remainder of Johnny's portion joined what Sid had already consumed.

" Father, we seed the mummers to-day ! They did fight with their swords an' they looked so grand with their ribbons an' bows an' rosettes. They fought till they killed each other dead. Were they really dead, father ? "

" No, my son, they was only playin'."

" An' was that really Father Christmas we seed ? "

" Yes, my son."

" How old is Father Christmas ? " persisted Johnny in his thin voice.

" Hunderds an' hunderds o' years old."

" Will he come tonight, father ? "

" Yes, my son, he'll be sure t' come."

" What, down chimney ? "

" Yes, down chimney."

" I'm glad there's plenty o' room for 'n. An' will he bring us all somethin' ? "

" Ah, he've a-got a good memory, an' so have I, for that matter. A good many Christmases I can mind, but the one I shall never forget was when I were a bwoy an' our old Uncle Ben sent the turkey. 'Twas mighty hard times we was livin' in an' my poor wold mother had nothin' for Christmas dinner an' a family of ten to provide for. 'Twas Christmas Eve, just as this mid be, and we was all a-sittin' round the vire when we heard a knockin' on the door. I can mind I ran and answered 'n bein' the eldest, and a boy handed in a girt parcel. I brought 'n in, put 'n on table for mother t' undo, an' there, avore our very eyes, were a turkey about the size of a young ostrich, all trussed up an' ready for bakin'."

" 'Tis from Uncle Ben," I said, " I know 'tis."

" Then I can mind how we all danced round table a-clappin' our hands."

" Good old Uncle Ben," we said. " Good old Uncle Ben," an' then I looked at mother, an' there she were a-wipin' 'er eyes wi' the corner o' 'er apron.

" ' Mother,' I zaid, ' What be cryin' for ? "

" ' For joy, my son,' she said, ' for joy.'

" Ah, that was a grand Christmas after all."

" Hark ! There's the waits, an' my favourite tuin."

The strains of " While shepherds watched " came with great gusto from beneath the window. As the last strain died away there came a thundering knock at the door.

" Tell 'em t' hit up another Sid, and their reward they shall have."

The latter obeyed and soon returned to inform the company that the choir would sing " Good Christian men, rejoice."

A slight scuffle of feet was heard without, a clearing of throats, with a few ahems, and the obliging choir struck up again with renewed vigour the requested carol, after which Bartholomew, not forgetting the promised reward, pronounced it time for bed.

" Mother, there," he added, in the manner of one concluding a speech of great import, " Who' d' say the least have done the most. All six puddin's she've a-made."

" No ! No ! We lent a hand, both Bess an' I. We've all a-stirred 'em up. Even Johnny there have gied a stir."

" Is the cake done, mother ? " enquired Sid.

" Ah, just out of oven an' pipin' hot."

" Then can I have a piece ? "

" What, on Christmas Eve ! What gluttons you be ! Off t' bed all o' 'ee. Father Christmas 'll soon be yer."

DORSET

'Tis 'ere that skies be bluer,
'Tis 'ere that birds zing zweet,
'Tis 'ere that maids be truer
Than any maids you meet.

'Tis 'ere that hearts be kinder
Though words, mid be, but vew
'Twas 'ere that I did vind 'er
As zweet as marnin' dew.

An' bless 'ee, she be neater
Than t'others iver be,
But ah ! 'er smile is zweeter
When she d' look on me.

Zoo 'ere we'll bide for iver,
'Till we've a-growd real old.
And 'ere we'll rest togither
Beneath the Darset mould.

POOLE

Wi' 'er waters round about 'er
Thease good old port d' stand,
Wi' narn so good a harbour
In all our native land.

An' up the busy High Street
The volks d' come for miles
To do their bit o' shoppin'
Wi' friendly nods an' smiles.

For Poole volk, they be kindly
The maidens trim an' neat
An' bless 'em, they be truer
Than any maids you meet.

Th' houses down on quayside
Be very, very old
An' date back 'vore th' Armada
Leastways, zo I'm told.

The Park d' take some beatin'
Wi' th' lakes and pretty vlowers,
An' volks d' watch the swans there
An' zit an' stroll ver hours.

An' zometimes out at Whitecliff
When the zun is in the West
I d' think I zee avore me
Th' Islands o' the Blest.

Ay, Poole's a grand old township
Wi' modest pride we boast
There's narn a town t' match it
The whole length o' th' coast.

POOLE FAIR

" 'Twill rain next week, fer sure," I zaid.
" Poole Vair d' start again,"
They'm puttin' up the jollities
Wi' all their might and main.

The round-abouts an' zwingin' boats
Be ready fer the vun,
The hooplas and the cokernuts
When yer day's work is done.

Walk up ! Walk up ! me fine young lads
Me pretty maidens too.
Poole Vair is on ! Poole Vair is on !
Especially fer you.

'Tis goin' t' be the best Poole Vair
That iver you can mind
Fer now that all the boys be back
We volk must treat 'em kind.

Walk up ! Walk up ! me fine young lads,
Me pretty maidens too.
Poole Vair is on ! Poole Vair is on !
An' lookin' out fer you.

A TREE

See in this unfrequented glade
The glory of the tree.
No lovelier thing God ever made,
Nor I, in fantasy.

I could not in my mind have thought
Such perfect symmetry,
Nor could I by the wise be taught
This handiwork I see.

Incarnate grandeur ! Dwarfing man
It stretches to the blue,
As lovely where no eye can scan
As here, to mortal view.

POOLE
DOWN ON THE QUAY
(FIFTY YEARS AGO)

Fifty years seems not a large span to have brought about so many changes. Yet, just half a century ago only sailing boats hove majestically into harbour, sometimes four abreast; coasters, schooners, brigantines, barques, briggs and barquentines, all manned by sailors who were in those days seamen indeed knowing every whim of the wind and weather.

From Sweden, Norway, Newfoundland and Russia, they came bearing their freights of timber, coal, ice, cranberries, salt fish and such-like commodities. There was no hurry in these times. A ship from Newfoundland would leisurely absorb the twelve months of the year, first in bringing her own cargo, then in reloading, ready to return at the caprice of the wind from whence she came. Her cargo of salt fish, which invariably arrived during the summer months, was unloaded by the help of local men and school-boys, the latter yaffeling (handing) them up to be stacked in hand-barrels at a shilling a day, later to be sold at a penny a pound.

They came and went, these stately little barques, whose seamen mingled with the natives of Poole in the jovial atmosphere of the "Hand-in-Hand" or "The Sailor's Home." Dotted along the quayside these little haunts of welcome waited. Here the seafarers told their tales and spat and drank and never a thought of enmity or war ruffled the philosophy of their uneventful lives.

Here, before the quay wall was built the water came twenty or thirty yards farther inland and the old 'box-houses,' whose little porches were built to protect them from wind and rain, were dotted along at the water's edge.

Here the school-boys watched the ships sailing into port and knew the flag of every vessel and the name of every sail. They grew up with the sea in their blood, so that when there was a call for sailors to supplement the crews Poole never lacked a volunteer.

In these days, too, the 'Oyster Bank,' like a miniature Chesil Beach lay surrounded by its little sea of mud some way from land. Across this intervening space, it has been said, a certain mad Army Oflicer, previously affected by sunstroke and clad in high boots swam his horse with a bunch of onions tied to its tail. Not content with this, he rode in the same hilarious fashion, up the high street, followed by crowds of small boys whooping with delight.

Down here on the quay, where school-boys worked for a shilling a day and men unloaded coal for a penny a ton, is the heart of Poole.

The Good Old Days! The Bad Old Days! Which were they?

Be it as it may there are those who, having survived from that time to this, still look back with a half-sigh for the colourful past.

THE DORSETSHIRE LAKE DISTRICT

Having recently visited the English Lake District I was able to make comparisons with our own miniature Lake District in Dorset and for beauty and colour, our liliputian pools on the heath, to my mind, tip the scales.

Admitting the grandeur, of course, of the Northern district, with its mountain scenery and its vast waters, there is about our own Lily Ponds an intimacy which makes them dear to every Dorset lover.

Impossible to explore all the lakes of the North in one day but, once having reached the vicinity of our own, within an hour or so, one can see the whole collection, these precious jewels set, not in 'a silver sea,' but in the brown and purple heath of the Hardy novels.

The first of the Lily Ponds is reached by tracking from Wareham about two miles over Stoborough and Creech Heath and then, unexpectedly, you come upon it.

The water, in colour, nearest approaches a turquoise, varying of course, according to the sky overhead. The sandy edge of the pond is faintly fringed with red, and there, in late

Summer and early Autumn, dotted about on the surface of the lake, are the lillies crimson, yellow, pink and white, all lying open to the sun.

How did they get there ? Were they wind-sewn from some nearby estate or did someone, long ago, deliberately scatter the seeds on the water to beautify these hidden pools ? No one knows, only that each little lake proudly bears its own array of brightly-coloured lilies, which lying there on the surface of the blue-green water, makes each pool a gem of beauty.

Here on the edge of the pond with the sand-martin cliffs behind you is an ideal spot for lunch. Here you will find a seclusion quite uninterrupted, for judging by the overgrown pathways on the heath, this ' pocket-sized ' edition of the lakes is very little known.

To reach the finest of the collection you climb up again and walk along the sand-hills to the Cotness Clay Workings, passing on your left another small pond sprinkled with lilies. If you follow the little mineral railway for a mile or so you come upon a lake, at once the largest and most beautiful of them all.

This one, like all the others, was originally a clay-pit dug by hands, which fact accounts for the delicate shades of colour the water assumes. Here the red-brown cliffs surrounding the pool are thickly wooded and provide a background which completes a picture of most enchanting beauty.

The lilies, too, are more numerous and varied in colour than on any of the other lakes, some pink and white, some a deep crimson, others shell pink, pure white or yellow.

Here, standing at the water's edge, one can view the whole of the lake with its wooded background mirrored in its waters, thus giving more satisfaction to the mind than all the wide stretches of the Northern lakes whose boundaries lie beyond the eye of the beholder.

If you can bear to leave, return along the mineral railway on to the Creech Heath once more, turning back now and again, if you will, to view the tree-clad hills in the far distance, giving the illusion of mountains in miniature and vying with the rugged peaks of Cumberland.

Eventually you cross over the road from Arne on your right, through the hamlet of Ridge, past an old farmhouse and so along the river bank, picturesque with its house-boats and barges, into Wareham again.

THE VILLAGE OF HAMMOON

About a mile and a half from Manston near Sturminster Newton, Hammoon is approached by an inviting little by-path forbidden to heavy vehicles on account of the light bridge over which the path leads into the village.

This little lane is a half-mile of verdant beauty in Summer with a profusion of wild flowers and undergrowth, made, no doubt, more luxuriant by previous winter floods.

Once over the bridge you turn the bend along the river bank into the village and view as pleasant a scene as is possible in rural England. In early Summer the water is low revealing the red-brown banks of the river, the fields lie out on either side golden with buttercups, the cows grazing peacefully, the ducks splashing in the water, and swans, with more dignity, gliding down stream. Hambledon Hill, now at your back as you enter the village, guards the smiling landscape.

Hammoon, although at one time much larger, is now a very small village consisting of the Church, Rectory and Manor, one or two farms, a handful of cottages and a few small houses. The place boasts of no post office, village hall or pub, the inhabitants depending either upon the " Plough " at Manston or the " Seymer Arms " at Shillingstone for their little social gatherings.

Now as you enter the village you see on your right the little thirteenth century Church known as St. Paul's which in its simplicity agrees well with its rustic surroundings.

It is in connection with the Church that we discover the origin of the name of the hamlet. It is given in Hutchins' ' History of Dorset ' that William de Moine came over with William the Conqueror with a retinue of forty-seven Knights in return for which he was given eleven manors in the county, the place in question being obviously one of them, for the name is derived from Ham, a Saxon word meaning dwelling, and Mohun or Moine the name of its liege-lord.

The Church, built seven hundred and more years ago, has, of course, been restored but retains much of its original character and distinction. It was when first constructed evidently much larger, as recent excavations have shown the foundations of a North Wing. Perhaps its most unusual features are the old wrought-iron stand next to the pulpit, which held the hour-glass used for timing sermons in the seventeenth century, and the "Devil's Door" which can be seen on the outside of the North Wall. The latter is now blocked up but the doorway was originally regarded as a means of escape for evil spirits which were supposed to have been released from infants during the Christening ceremony. The door was left open during the service for this purpose. The 'lepers squint' too may be traced on the outside of the North Wall and level with the top of the South door are the markings of the old Mass Dial which was used in Medieval times as a kind of sun-dial to time the services.

Another remarkable feature of the Church is the beautifully carved reredos under the East window. This is a rare example of medieval sculpture in local stone, the centre panel representing the crucifixion and those on either hand, three Apostles. Traces of paint may be seen in the crevices giving some idea of its original striking beauty. A simple painted wood moulding now surrounds the sides and top thus enclosing this gem of antiquity.

The Priest's door may be observed on the North side of the Chancel. By this door the priest in ancient days entered from his dwelling on the South side of the Church. The house still stands although now has been extended on either side and appears to-day as a picturesque cottage fronted by an old-world garden.

It is interesting to note, that in common with all Churches before the Reformation, this little edifice was the centre of the life of the village. The nave and porch was the principle meeting place. Here the villagers met to transact their business either of legal or commercial nature. Thither they fled for refuge in times of war or peril of any description and here goods were probably stored and possibly bales of wool at the time of the great wool trade in the fifteenth century.

Leaving the Church you come to the Rectory, modern and somewhat incongruous, standing between the former and the Manor.

The Manor in all probability is older than the Church since Mohun possessed it in Domesday Book. However, the massive oak studded door is similar to that of the Church, indicating that it is of more or less the same period. The porch, beautifully carved, has a little chamber above it which is characteristic of the earliest manors of this country.

The interior has been to a great extent preserved intact through-out the centuries. The enormous open fireplace still stands at one end of what was once the vast hall of the Manor, where in Medieval times the whole village sat at meat and were employed according to their varying abilities by the Lord of the Manor.

Formerly there was a corresponding fireplace at the other end of the hall but this has been blocked up and the room divided into two compartments. It is not difficult to imagine the assembled companies of centuries ago being entertained on festive occasions in the original hall by wandering minstrels and jesters, for then the village was one community devoid of class distinction and innocent of competitive ambition.

During recent excavations the painting of the original Court room in the East wing has been revealed showing the one-time glory and importance of this beautiful Dorset manor.

Until comparatively recent years the village green lay immediately opposite the building and here the village made merry with May-pole and Folk dancing, but, I am told, the villagers' goats strayed and cropped the grass, in consequence of which a certain arbitrary liege-lord enclosed the green.

Hammoon has, in common with most villages, lost perhaps its perfect entity. The old villagers have died out and the modern spirit has produced an independence of each other amongst the present day inhabitants. There remains, however, the kindliness and hospitality and their pride of this time-honoured village which lies so peacefully beside the River Stour.

SPRING RAMBLE TO CHAPMAN'S POOL

We started off at the reasonable hour of 10.27 a.m. from Poole station having booked our fares for Corfe Castle.

No matter how many times one visits this little place it never loses its appeal. It has an air of peace and restfulness that even the menace of war could not dispel. It delights the eye and satisfies the senses, giving out a welcome to all and sundry. Even the castle ruins seem to nod in friendly fashion from its perch on the little green hill.

We left Corfe and struck out over the common, knowing full well that before the day was out we should see it again. The common was ablaze with gorse, the trees and bushes varying shades of tender green, interspersed with the virginal whiteness of the hawthorn. Overhead the sky was a cloudless blue and the cuckoo called, presumably only that we might be aware of his presence.

Looking back, there was Corfe again nestled at the bottom of the hill. We could see its long street overlooked by the ruin. " A funny little place " one of our party remarked, but this was surely the kind of raillery one keeps for one's best-loved friends, bespeaking in actuality a warm attachment.

We took our way from the common through a bluebell wood. The branches hung low overhead and a stream dawdled to the left of us. Ferns grew in profusion on the banks and the bluebells formed a misty blue carpet giving out a sweet scent that filled the air.

Straightening our backs and vaulting a stile, we were out again into the open fields and so into another stretch of common, with Kingston in the valley on our right. Its two churches could be discerned amongst the trees but the village itself was hidden from view.

Here we got on to the main road and headed for Worth Matravers. Missing now the shade of the trees we were in the full glare of the noonday sun and by the time we reached the village were ready for a halt for lunch.

The " Star and Compass " is all that a country inn could be and "Mine Host " a friendly soul. Folks had congregated outside as well as in this inviting establishment. It seems the local artist sees fit to frequent this place and his paintings adorn the walls of the interior.

The church, too, with its Norman Arch and stained glass windows is pleasing to the eye and suggestive of the quiet worship of the village folk.

But Worth was not our objective, so refreshed, we started off again over more stretches of common to Chapman's Pool. Here we dabbled in the water and lazily contemplated the peaceful cove. The intense blue of the sky gave to the natural greyness of the rocks a softer hue and the sea lay out before us serene and calm. The place was almost deserted, on account, no doubt, of its being somewhat difficult of access, but hardy walkers like ourselves felt amply rewarded for our efforts. We dared not linger here as the last train from Corfe left soon after six. So we once more started off prepared for the uphill climb to Kingston.

About mid-way between Chapman's Pool and this village we struck through a natural valley displaying the typical unspoilt beauty of the English countryside. Here truly was a very paradise. All the delights and promises of spring were thus lavishly displayed to gladden the eyes and hearts of all beholders.

We reached Kingston somewhat travel-stained, glad now of the descent into Corfe where tea awaited us. And Corfe, like all true friends, made us welcome again although for one whole day we had turned our backs upon her and cast admiring glances at other fair sights.

We had tea in the Tudor Cafe. Never did cream and jam and scones taste better and never was a cup of tea more welcome.

AUTUMN RAMBLE TO WOOLSBARROW

We took a Bere Regis 'bus and alighted at the "Baker's Arms." From there, walked through the village of Organford and across the wind-swept heath to the little known vantage point of Woolsbarrow.

The view from there was wonderful. Corfe Castle stood out clearly in a gap between the hills and all around for miles stretched the familiar Dorset landscape of wooded hill and dale. We lunched in a chalk-pit on Woolsbarrow at peace with the world. Descending from here we discovered we were overlooking a valley rivalling the beauty of Scottish scenery with its rugged hills, and mists, indeed, we found this portion of landscape to be appropriately named "Little Scotland."

We then took off towards the picturesque village of East Bloxworth, and from thence on to the delightful roadway leading to Bloxworth proper. We viewed the church with the now disused hour-glass on the pulpit and noted the expansive pew allotted to squire and family which boasted a stove and a carpet.

Just outside Bloxworth we struck into the Bere woods and soon noted what must be the largest oak in the district; we measured its diameter with a walking stick and judged it to be at least twelve feet across.

About two miles from here we came out to Woodbury Hill, still the site of the annual fair as in the days of Thomas Hardy. The vans, new and brightly painted stood in readiness for the great day and called to mind the motley crowd which peopled this hill-top and disported themselves so freely, differently clad but similarly minded in the days of long ago.

The rest of the way we took through the woods, the heather now pale mauve around us, the bracken a golden brown and the turf, soft and springy under our feet. At length we reached Bere Regis, partook of a generous tea at the Royal Oak, then visited, as is our wont, the village church. This church, with its magnificent roof is well enough known to need no description, but a tribute must be paid to the gallant bell-ringers who allowed us to watch their efforts in the belfry.

They rang a peal right merrily, then, during a pause, they voiced what was in all our minds : " War—or Peace ? "

Said one of the ringers : " Parson gave out last week, Harvest Festival next Sunday, if . . . . . "

Two vegetable marrows were already in the church below. I hope they will not wait in vain for the rest of the bounty which bespeaks the goodness of God.

THE GREAT FROST OF 1890

We think if we get a cold snap we are having a hard winter, but in comparison with some of the winters of fifty-odd years ago we scarcely know what cold weather is.

I was talking the other day to an old Dorset man who could remember the Great Frost of 1890, when the River Stour was frozen to a depth of eleven inches. Layers of snow between the frosts helped, of course, to give the depth, and the river, at all times a centre of attraction, became now the pivot around which evolved the activity and merriment of whole parishes along its banks.

For the length of a mile, folks could skate, slide, walk, dance or toboggan as they chose. In fact the river became a highway and a scene of such merriment which has surely never been known since.

To show how firmly established was this kingdom of ice, a " Four-in-hand " was drawn on to the lake in Poole Park and remained there in solitary state until signs of a thaw appeared.

Near the town of Sherborne, an ox was roasted whole over a lake without impairing the ice, and distributed amongst the inhabitants the next day.

The Christmas of 1890 was most certainly a white one and Shakespeare's well-known lines, " milk comes frozen home in pail " were daily exemplified. The farmers in this locality had, at milking time, first to find their cows buried in the heavy fall of snow. They called them by name until they moved and so betrayed their whereabouts, then, as they milked, the liquid froze on the edge of the pail.

Sheep lay helplessly buried till dug out. Horses on the way to the smithy to be "roughed" had their feet tied up in bags to prevent slipping. Cows, less sure-footed than horses, slipped on the glassy roads and had to be held down by the neck as bags were tied on their feet to get them up again.

Cider froze in barrels in the cellars. It was indeed a frigid world

People worked hard during the day-time so that when night came they could give themselves up to enjoyment. Chinese lanterns were strung over the river in a small Dorset town, the Band played the latest ditties and the whole population joined in this Carnival on the ice. They decked themselves in fancy dress and danced till mid-night beneath the railway bridge, the quiet Vale of Blackmore, the unaccustomed scene of their merriment.

For six long weeks the frost held and my informant tells me that, as a lad, he spent so much time on the ice that some local, beholding him scuttling down the river, remarked, "I should think thee must be zick o' it!"

But he most surely was not, nor any of the other revellers, for they skated, danced and played till the night before the thaw.

OLD DORSET SUPERSTITIONS

Few of us, although we may not care to admit it, really like to upset salt, walk under a ladder or make up the thirteenth at a party, but these little whims, of course, are nothing in comparison with the superstitions which were common in this county less than fifty years ago.

In the village of Lulworth, round about this time, the dead were often buried with a penny in one hand and a hammer in the other; the penny, we presume, as the entrance fee to heaven and the hammer to raise the coffin lid. When one lay dying, the doors and windows were left open to ensure an easier passage into the next world, while the pillow of the one about to depart was stuffed with pigeon's feathers.

Witches, of course, were believed to exist as recently as 1908 and a family then living five miles from Dorchester were reputed to inherit qualities of witchcraft. In 1901, an old Dorset woman, on being accused of being a witch replied, " Well, as folks do say, I mid be a witch, but not such a girt one as my mother were."

Another superstition which persisted many years later was that the globules of grease formed from the guttering of a candle (resembling coffin handles) were supposed to foretell a death in the family and with this in mind, an old Dorset farmer suddenly stopped during the singing of a hymn in Chapel, where his daughter was playing the harmonium. He had noticed that the candle had guttered and formed the ominous coffin handles. The daughter, noting what had happened, hastily pinched them off and the old man resumed his song of praise.

This same farmer, we are told, in his youth paid a visit to a " wise man " to ask his advice about a litter of pigs which were ailing. The " wise man " informed him that the pigs were being " overlooked " and as a corrective supplied him, for a modest fee, with a powder which was to be burnt in the fire after the house was shut up for the night. As a result, blue flames went up the chimney, knocks were heard from without and next morning the piglets were found to be in perfect health.

A man from Winterbourne Houghton is reported to have borne testimony to the spell cast upon him by a witch, whom he had displeased by refusing to pay money which she had demanded. She decreed that from that time forward he would be cursed with ill luck and that " horses would bring him to ruin." Funnily enough, soon after, one of his horses died and within a few weeks the others followed suit. This continued till he became a ruined man as predicted, and could buy no more. One morning, from his window, he saw his son's horse, dragging a load of faggots down the hill, take fright. He ran to the rescue, was knocked down and fatally injured.

Any untimely conduct of beasts and birds was conside an evil omen : for example, the tapping of a bird on the window pane or the crowing of a cock at an unusual hour. One old country woman was heard to remark, ' If the cock do crow after twelve o'clock noon, her is doing it to bring I bad news, or John may be bad agean. I can't a-bear to hear 'n." It may be remembered that Dairyman Crick notes with foreboding the cock crowing at noon on the departure of Tess and Angel Clare on their ill-fated honeymoon at Wellbridge.

Bees swarming on the branch of a tree or apple-blossom flowering out of season were also considered bad omens.

There is a story told of a Portland man who woke at midnight aware of two figures standing on either side of him. A voice warned him that his time to depart this world had come. Filled with terror he begged for mercy, saying that he was not yet ready to die. He was granted twelve hours' grace. The man set out for work next day. Towards noon he went on an errand but before the last stroked of twelve had sounded he had breathed his last.

Faith in dreams as a foretelling of the future was very strong. Here is one example given as authentic : a Dorset woman dreamt three times that her husband had cut his arm in an accident. She informed him of her dream and after the last repetition of it, gave him " a roll of white rag " to take with him to work, " in case anything happened." After their morning of mowing grass, the labourers sat down to their " nunch " and the man related to the others his wife's dream. On rising he trod on his scythe which flew up and cut his arm, so fulfilling to the letter the prediction of the dream.

So one might sight a hundred fancies and superstitions of early days.

THE CLUB WALK

Manston was all alive with excitement. It was the day of " The Annual Club Walk." All the village prepared to make merry, and only a few dissenters would be out of the fun. It was pre-eminently a Church affair, but some of the more broad-minded chapel-goers joined in the procession and the merry-making in the evening.

The Maypole and the round-abouts were sufficient to convince some of the more devout brethren that the devil was afoot amongst them. Accordingly they gave the whole affair a wide berth, some treking as far as Hambledon Hill, to avoid any contamination from the revelry of the godless. These sainted ones held up their hands in pious horror at the drunkenness and brawling which was the inevitable climax of these occasions.

The little girls appeared on the day of the " Club Walk " with clean starched white frocks, embroidered white petticoats peeping out from below, and hair " crimped " for the occasion. Their elder sisters, with motive more subtle, used all the arts of which they were capable to enhance their appearance. With ribbons and frills and flounces they bedecked their youthful persons. They adjusted their bonnets at the most coquettish angles and wore a bouquet to give an air of festivity. For in the evening every Jack would find a Jill, and it would be shame indeed if a maid came home alone. Her more successful sisters would point at her the finger of scorn.

" On the shelf, that's what you be," they would say.

The procession headed by the Sturminster brass band started off in fine style, the club members wearing their colours and their banners flying. They made a complete circuit of the parish, pausing at remote farms to play a lively tune, but first they marched to the Church, and heard the specially appointed vicar give his discourse on the " sick and needy." That over, the rest of the day was given up to merriment. The band struck up and their spirits rose. They played a tune at each of the farms and were handed out a mug of cider for their entertainment. An air of revelry prevailed. The sun shone down in all its glory and the exertion of walking and playing the instruments caused some members of the band to be much over-heated. The perspiration was visible on their faces and they mopped their brows at intervals with their handkerchiefs. After the procession they proceeded to Farmer Barrabell's twelve-acre field where the marquees and fun fair were installed.

The dinner looked appetising enough with generous helpings of cold meats placed ready for consumption. Pickles of different varieties gave piquancy to the meals and beer and ale were cheap and plentiful.

Several important looking carriages outside the tent indicated the arriavl of the grandees. The working people were proud to sit at meat with the Squire, Vicar and Doctor of the parish. These august personages were the patrons of the Club, and the poor people looked to them for guidance in matters of organisation. Dinner over, speeches were made and the people applauded the Vicar's praise of the Club and its work in the vicinity. He lauded the Church and praised God for the harmonious gathering of rich and poor alike ; the squire and the working man partaking from the same table.

Now for the rest of the afternoon and evening all entered with zest into the various amusements. The club walk was the greatest event of the year in Manston. It was the only occasion on which the whole village went gay. There were sports of every description, egg-and-spoon races, sack races, and the greasy pole ; the one that caused the most amusement being the Singing Contest. Anyone could enter this competition. You were enjoined to sing a comic song right through without laughing, having at the same time a pig under your arm. Several of the bolder spirits started off valiantly but collapsed when the pig began to squeal and twist about. At length, one solemn looking farmer took the pig, adjusted it firmly under his arm and sang from beginning to end as though he were stranger to a smile or popular comic song.

There was Maypole dancing in the field and it was a pretty sight to see the lightly clad boys and girls tripping over the grass to the fiddler's tune. They had practised at the Vicarage for weeks beforehand, much to the disgust of the chapel folks who considered that anything in the shape of dancing savoured of the devil. As they danced, the girls' long hair flowed out behind them and their lithe bodies moved with unconscious grace in and out, over and under, the gaily coloured ribbons.

After tea the majority of the men folk had no other ambition than to refill their cups and mugs. There was a huge barrel of beer in the marquee and if that failed, " The Plough " was close at hand. Their hands were unsteady now, and the passage of the mug to the lips was made in small uneven jerks. But the liquid seemed aware of its final destination and found its way, like the river to the sea, and little was spilt despite the condition of the drinkers.

The Country dancing was held in an enclosure, the space being portioned off by hurdles. Considering the unevenness of the ground the dancers conducted themselves admirably. The lads of the village could tread a measure neatly enough, and the lasses looked sprightly and dainty in their frilly white gowns. By the look of things most of the girls had found themselves partners and were well pleased with their selection. One or two lingered on the edge of the enclosure, either too shy to push themselves forward or less attractive to the male eye. It may have been that the girls looked their prettiest on that day, or it may have been the magic of a June evening, but it was a certain thing that more matches were made at the club fete than at any other time during the year. The young men betrayed their intentions by a questing look in the eye, an alertness and a sizing-up quality when the maidens were in sight. The maidens betrayed their consciousness by side-long glances and coquettish smiles. The boldest stared and the modest blushed. Few were disappointed for cupid was busy indeed.

The club walk fete would soon be over and the villagers would have to wait another twelve months before they would make merry again. Small wonder that they were out to extract the last atom of enjoyment they could out of the day's programme.

Many of the maidens depended upon this day as their best opportunity throughout the year of displaying their charms before an assembly of young men. Many couples, now happily married, had met as total strangers at some distant club fete.

CHRISTMAS IN OLD POOLE

Things were very different in Poole sixty years ago from what they are now.

Though money was scarce, prices were low and food plentiful, and I've no doubt the children who swarmed in the alley-ways around the Quay looked forward to christmas as much as the children of to-day.

With oranges forty a shilling and nuts sixpence a pound, their stockings were tolerably filled.

Most of the families mustered a roast dinner with plum pudding after, and if some of the poorer ones had to be content with only a long look in the toy-shop windows they were strangely content. Their eyes feasted upon the clock-work figures with their queer contortions and the various toys on view ; then they went away feeling they had had their lawful share.

Then there was the furmity. This commodity, made from flour, water, spice and raisins or currants, was very much in demand. The raisins in the process of cooking " plimmed " to three times their normal size and were known to the locals as " Cock Whollopers."

" Granny Long " kept a little emporium near the Quay where she weighed up tea and sugar, sold cooked peas and pigs' feet and half-penny-worths of baked ' teaties '.

On Christmas Eve she ladled out steaming hot furmity and sold it to anyone so minded for a halfpenny or penny as the case may be.

Many of these street arabs were glad to get out of the cold into a warm room where they could sit and consume on the premises this Yuletide gruel and at the same time torment " Granny Long " as opportunity occurred.

They would, after chewing a pig's foot, throw the bones at the empty canisters which adorned the shelves, causing " Granny " to jump round in alarm from her preoccupation with the furmity.

Then, waiting for her back to be turned again, they would drop a bit of candle in the peas which happened to be cooking, or perform any other such monkey tricks as came to their minds.

Wise to her tormentors, she would sometimes try to shut the door upon them as they came for a halfpenny-worth or penny-worth of furmity, but clogging the door with an intruding foot they foiled her attempts.

On rare occasions when her patience had reached its limit she would brandish a knife about the shop, driving the interlopers out then lock the door upon them and do herself out of the evening's custom.

Fortunate for them and all concerned that no one adulterated the furmity with rum as did the hag who served Michael Henchard, the " Mayor of Casterbridge." The latter, Hardy relates, after a number of such " lacings," became thoroughly bemused and sold his wife to a sailor in the company for the sum of £5.

Round about this time, too, the mummers made their rounds from one public house to another, and children waited to catch sight of them as they came from " The Jolly Sailor," " The Steam Packet," " The Sailor's Home," " The Lord Nelson " or " The Hand and Heart," as the case may be.

Gaily clad in bright-coloured cambric and top hats, carrying tambourines, trumpets, and various musical instruments, they went from one local to the other singing, reciting or acting.

Some featured notable figures in history such as Lord Nelson or the Duke of Wellington and were dressed accordingly. Father Christmas, of course, was included too.

These mummers date right back to medieval times and began as a religious ritual performed by monks and nuns, then later developed into pageants and ridings to stimulate historic imagination. They, in effect, proved the mainstream of the drama proper.

Hardy gives an adequate description of the mummers in "The Return of the Native," when Eustacia Vye usurps the part of a Turkish knight in the play "Saint George" in order that she might obtain a closer view of Clym Yeobright, at whose house the mummers were to perform.

Returning to Christmas time in Poole, butchers were very much to the fore. A week or so before the festival the prize cattle adorned with their rosettes were driven around the town for all to view, then killed and hung intact for the Butchers' Show Day a week before Christmas.

In those days a pork butcher *was* a pork butcher and did not harbour a conglomeration of fruit, vegetables and tinned stuffs. In Harriss' shop (now taken over by Millers) you could obtain ham, smoked and cured, for 11d. a lb.!

Christmas Eve was entirely given up to merry-making of an innocent though somewhat boisterous nature, for the lads of the locality paraded the streets at intervals the whole night through singing songs and carols undeterred by the police.

Some carried their enthusiasm as far as Bournemouth and sang in the bandstand of the arcade. These, of course, were only those who possessed voices of true musical quality and their performance required some rehearsing before they favoured the aristocratic neighbouring town with their nativity songs.

RUSTIC TRANSPORT

Some fifty-odd years ago transport was slow, albeit picturesque.

The farm-hand, paid, perhaps, 4d. a week, besides his daily portion of bread-and-cheese and his initial suit of corduroy, drove his leige-lord's fat cattle from Hammoon, near Sturminster Newton to Poole, where they were put on barges to be conveyed to Portsmouth.

He trudged on foot every inch of the way, his pockets so light that in one instance, having delivered himself of his cattle, and at the same time his last copper, he was unable to pay the halfpenny toll at the old Hamworthy bridge. In consequence he dodged past the toll keeper and forced his weary feet to run chased by the keeper till he was safely out of reach.

A working woman of those days thought nothing of carrying a child " pick-a-back " from Sturminster Newton Common to Poole, a distance of about twenty-five miles. There was for her, no other means of transport.

These travellers on the road had eyes to see the elusive " Jack-o-Lantern " which haunted the marshy places and hopped like an illuminated frog by the river-side.,

Does the " Will-o'-the-wisp " still dance in watery places at the fall of the year ? Presumably so, unless he has withdrawn from the stage since there is no gallery to applaud.

Another familiar sight at this time was the little two-wheeled covered pony-cart which was driven regularly by an old man accompanied by his wife, from Sturminster Newton to Poole, conveying " lollipops " and brandy-balls to the Poole shops.

The old couple, nick-named Mr. and Mrs. Popsey, made these sweets themselves, wholesome and gaily coloured. They filled tins and jars, loaded their rustic conveyance and started off at two or three o'clock in the morning, relying solely upon their little white pony to cover the miles which lay between them and their destination.

It was an epic occasion when the old Hamworthy bridge was opened for a barge to go under when the old couple were on it, complete with their pony-cart, lollipops and all.

As the bridge was opened they went down—and landed intact on the passing barge, none the worse for their sudden and unexpected transport to the water-way below.

BIRD STARVIN'

" BIRD STARVIN' "

Either we have become more humane in our attitude towards the birds, or we now attach more importance to the knowledge acquired in school-desks than to that which is gleaned from nature itself. Whichever may be the case " Bird Starvin' " as an occupation has now become extinct and each year, as the corn ripens, the birds are allowed, unmolested, to eat their fill of the ripening crops, and no small boys are employed to frighten them off. The scare-crow, of course, is still to be seen keeping his lonely vigil after the corn has been cut, but no other means is now adopted to keep the birds from their meals.

Until an old Dorset man told me of his experiences as a boy at " Bird Starvin'," I had imagined this a most joyless and uninteresting pursuit, imposed as a sort of punishment upon unwilling lads who would much rather have been at play. This idea was, no doubt, engendered by Hardy's conception of the lonely boy Jude, who, in the extreme sensitivity of his nature allowed the birds to eat their fill when he was paid to frighten them off, for which offence he was thrashed to within an inch of his life.

Now, however, I know that the boys of fifty years ago used to look forward to the weeks in early Spring and from the end of July till the beginning of September, when " Bird Starvin' " was required, as the happiest days of all the year. They went out armed with buckets and sticks or wooden clappers, and food sufficient for their needs from early in the morning till the setting of the sun. Whole fields of corn were at their disposal, for as long as they kept up the rattle and noise between them they could take turns to go off birds' nesting, see-sawing, swinging or any other delightful pastime the season offered. A plank of wood through a fivebarred gate made an excellent see-saw ; a swing could easily be attached to the overhanging bough of a tree and, as for birds' nesting, they were able during these weeks to collect innumerable specimens of eggs and, like the little Hiawatha, ' Knew of every birds its language '. They knew the haunts of jackdaws in hollow trees, and magpies in the " thornin' " bush, so carefully covered in with a roof over the nest. They knew, too, how to distinguish between the rooks' and crows' nests. While the rooks built right at the top of the elms, the crows made their nests in the " verks " (forks) of the trees lower down. But rooks or crows, it made no difference to them, for with all the agility of their " ancestors " they climbed to the top of the tree, and robbed the nests. Hawks' and owls' they pilfered, too, and every kind of bird they came across always with the exception of the robin. This latter bird was as sacred to them as the cow to the Hindu. They never touched a robin's egg. Not, we presume, that they were afraid of having crooked fingers, as was then supposed, but just that they felt it in their bones that you mustn't harm a robin.

Then, of course, there were the moorhens. These brown-spotted eggs were of a reasonable size, and whilst some of the boys were scaring off the ever recurring flock of birds the others gathered sufficient sticks to make a fire, procured water from a near-by spring and boiled the eggs in an old saucepan, which they had smuggled out unknown to their parents. They took good care, of course, to make the fire near a gateway, to avoid mishap, and there enjoyed the meal they had found, as did their forbears of the primeval forests, who hunted down their prey at somewhat greater risks.

So much were these " bird starvers " envied by their contemporaries that now and again a boy would play truant from school and join in the merry-makers escaping punishment on the plea of having been out Bird Starvin'.

In these ways, then, did the boys who were sent out to scare the birds from the corn at 4d. or 6d. a day while away the sunny hours. They had, of course, to provide for rain, and for this emergency rigged up a house of sticks and grass, and took it in turns to creep inside, whilst the others rattled away the persistent birds. Sundays and week-days alike they continued their watch, till the day came at length when the last sheaf of corn was gathered in, and the fields bereft of their golden produce. The boys themselves, as the fruit of their labours, would have in their possession a collection of birds' eggs of every possible variety, which they had first blown and then lovingly threaded on a piece of string. These they kept at home till it was the time for " bird starvin' " again.

THE UNLOVED SOCIETY

Forty summers ago, the members of the Workmen's Club, or as it was commonly called, the Dog's Hole, disported themselves in many a pleasure trip and moonlight excursion. The latter was a popular diversion and cost each member the modest sum of ninepence.

On one such occasion a party of young men and women, as many as two hundred strong, started away at seven in the morning and left Bournemouth aboard *The Lord Elgin* (still in existence to-day, carrying commodities to the Isle of Wight) and sailed for Swanage Bay.

The trip over the placid sea was unalloyed pleasure. The St. James's town band, which accompanied them, played the latest ditties whilst some danced and others lazed as became their respective dispositions.

One young man whose contentment had reached its zenith in blissful sleep, was made the target of the idlers. A monkey-on-a-stick was produced by someone in the party, placed in the crook of the sleeping man's arm, the cameraman called for and the picture taken. Of these harmless operations the sleeping man knew nothing till presented several days later with his undisputable likeness.

By the time they reached Swanage pier they could well have done without the band for the youths of the party, intoxicated by nothing more than their own high spirits filled the air with song. One, more adventurous than the rest, stood on the bridge of the boat to conduct the performance whilst his comrades' lusty voices united in such spirited airs as " The Belle of New York " and " The Greek Slave ". Such was the lilt of their songs in the moonlight, that though the Swanage Regatta was in full swing folks came away from other attractions to join in.

Indeed so much were these youths addicted to song that it happened on one of their trips to Studland when they entered the little village Church, the same adventurous spirit who conducted the band on Swanage pier mounted the pulpit and gave out a hymn. All the company joined in and, although not quite as out-of-place as Hardy's Melstock Choir who fiddled a dance in the midst of a service, they nevertheless at the vicar's sudden appearance melted away.

In one direction, however, the Workmen's Club was less successful. Having seen an advertisement in *The Morning Leader* to the effect that a certain young woman sought correspondence with an eligible young man between the ages of nineteen and thirty, they each, unknown to the other, made application. It afterwards leaked out that, although the young woman herself received a shower of letters, the eligible young man received no replies at all. Thereafter, they christened themselves the ' Unloved Society '.

THE GOOD OLD DAYS OF METHODISM

A great religious revival had sprung up in Sturminster and its vicinity. Meetings were held every night, and added to the usual numbers of chapel-goers were a number of interested and over-awed spectators. They were told with conviction that hell-fire was the portion of those who did not believe. Many by the magnetic power of the evangelist were compelled to confess their sins and announce themselves converts to the Saving Faith. Nightly the numbers increased and sinners tumbled out to the Altar rails kneeling in contrition before God. Religious fervour and excitement ran high and the more excitable among the brethren shouted, laughed and wept in an effort to proclaim the Saving Grace.

Among the most noted of the fresh converts were three youths who had hitherto been regarded as being outside the pale of Gospel influence. They had been great and untiring drinkers, they swore, smoked and gambled, in fact they did everything that the Methodist Church taught was wordly and evil. But now, the strongest spirit of the three having pronounced himself duly saved and cleansed, the other two followed suit. They were seen, therefore, visiting remoted country villages, with Bible under arm, walking perhaps as much as twenty miles to spread the glorious news of Salvation.

One night the three were to hold forth in a small village chapel about five miles out. Knowing that, in their fresh enthusiasm, they were likely to over-step their allotted time for speaking, they agreed to place a watch on the ledge of the pulpit and to portion themselves each ten minutes. The first two, guided by the timepiece, managed to pour forth their eloquence in the space of ten minutes, without mishap. The last to speak having suppressed his emotion for a considerable time longer than the others burst out into such a flood of rapture as could only be expressed by violent gesticulation of the arms and thumping of the pulpit ledge. In consequence, before his time was up the watch, by virtue of a vigorous thump from clenched fist in its near vicinity, jumped from its perch on the pulpit ledge clean into the midst of upturned faces in the congregation and landed with a resounding thud on the bare floor. For a moment there was silence, then a voice said " carry on, brother, 'tis the Lord's will. What do we want wi' watches, the time is the Lord's."

" Amen," said another in a high-pitched voice. " Bless 'is Name ! If we d' bide till dark, he'll guide us hwome."

One night several of the well-versed Methodists were appointed to stay behind after a meeting to assist brothers and sisters groping after the light to find salvation. Quite a number of the congregation remained behind to receive instruction. One old man was particularly impervious to the proffered Grace, and incapable of understanding the theology, simple as it was.

" What be I t' do ? What be I t' do ? " he questioned repeatedly.

" Believe on the Lord Jesus Christ, and you shall be saved," his wiser brother admonished.

" I don't zee it," complained the seeker after salvation.

With that the other lifted his hand and gave him a resounding smack across the cheek. " Now, can 'ee zee it ! " he said. But then, in the words of one of the other brethren, " If 'ee 'aint got all his wits, the pore feller cain't be expected t' zee it ; he'll be made allowances for, I don't doubt."

One morning a little group, standing in the market-place of Sturminster, talked over the great meeting of the night before, while the air was still highly-charged with the electricity of soul-saving grace.

"Did 'ee 'ear John Trollop zay as 'ow 'ee were converted?" said one called Hayter, addressing the company. "I 'eard 'n zay that avore a' were saved, as soon as he did come hwome, the cat did scurry off out, but now 'ee d' cock up his tail and come straight up to 'n. He d' purr and look up into 'is faece as much as t' zay, 'You be a changed man!'"

"Ah! and a changed man 'ee be," chimed in a woman of the group, "used to knock 'is wife about and come hwome drunk, now a' don't touch a drap. Ah! 'tis the power o' the Gospel."

The incidents here related are taken from actual fact, in a West country revival.

LIZER ANN

Eliza Ann Blake, known to all her compatriots as "Lizer Ann" kept a lodging house, wherein she sheltered any stray tramp or vagabond for ninepence a night. It was a rest house, and port of call for the army of ne'er do wells, who frequented the roads. "Lizer Ann's" tumble-down shanty was better than the workhouse; a fellow could keep his 'baccy' there and no one would force him into a bath. For close on fifty years Eliza Ann had lived there, first with her own children, and now with grand-children as well. They played contentedly, with swarms of other unkempt mites, in the yard, around which the condemned dwellings clustered.

There were several of these tumble-down shanties besides Eliza's, all of which were unfit for habitation. The thatched roofs were falling in and when it rained the women folk would fetch their pails and stand them beneath the holes in the roof to catch the water. In hot weather the area reeked with the smell of dirt and bad drainage. Cleanliness was unthought of and neglect was apparent everywhere. One might well ask where Liza Ann slept all her family as well as her boarders.

They must have lain anywhere, content that a roof sheltered them, at least to a certain extent. It was somewhere to 'turn in' when the weather was cold or inclement.

In spite of her loud voice and bustling manner, there was about Liza Ann, something defenceless, and you may be sure that many of Liza's casuals never paid her a penny. She was good-natured and kindly beneath her coarse exterior and self-seeking never. This, no doubt accounted for the fact that on every Guy Fawkes' night, the lads of the area contrived to make a guy which, funnily enough, resembled Liza Ann. On one occasion the guy was crowned with Liza's old hat, and she herself was in the forepart of the procession, showing that, unlike her betters, she cared nothing for ridicule and was a stranger to resentment. Here was a woman who could in no wise stand up for her rights and, having no husband, she became the butt for any ill humour or coarse rag that might be in progress.

Then came the day when Liza Ann was told to go. The dwellings were condemned and were to be pulled down. Unquestioningly and without protest Eliza Ann packed up her few belongings ; and with the aid of her sons got them to the strange place, where they had offered her a two-roomed cottage. No one knew the heart-break or the wrench for Eliza Ann. She expressed no word of regret at leaving the hovel which was her kingdom. She had been rooted there, the squalor and the dirt she had never heeded, but the communal existence had been her delight. Now she was to go away into a strange place, where she could never take root again. She would miss the morning's gossip with arms akimbo, in the yard. She would shelter no more unfortunates on the road ; there would be strange faces and strange voices round about her. No other air could give her life for long, but Eliza Ann made no complaint. When the last of her belongings had gone and the youngest of the children hoisted into the wagon, that would take them away, Eliza took one last look at the place she had called her home for so long, then she slowly mounted and as the wagon moved away Eliza looked in front of her with unseeing eyes. Seeing the old woman's stony countenance, one of the children hid her face against her apron and whimpered.

" Grannie, why be us goin' away ? " she asked.

For answer Eliza stroked her head, but no words came. The wagon rumbled on ; they were going away but Eliza had left her heart in the tumble-down dwelling, that was condemned as unfit for habitation.

A SHOT IN THE DARK

It was a funny thing but if anything went wrong in the village it was always " Varmer John " they sent for.

One time it was on account of an old man taken with delirium tremens. He was a big, gaunt fellow, twice the size of " Varmer John," vowing murder to anyone who came near him, but John had pinned down his arms and held him thus, till all the blue devils had disappeared.

Another time a workman was trapped in a foul well and they had asked for volunteers to go down. Farmer John had gone down and pulled him up, at the risk of his own life. But it was when he shot the mad dog that " Varmer John" became immortal although it was meant to be a secret.

It was dead of night and John was asleep ; came a thundering knock at the door. It was repeated before John thrust his head out of the window.

" 'Tis on'y I," came a voice. " There's a mad dog about, mad's ever can be. Will 'ee come out an' shoot 'n ? "

" But I've never handled a gun in my life," replied the young farmer, "except on a fair-day ! "

" Never mind about that," the voice answered, " If you don't shoot 'n fust time, you can try agen."

His eyes now accustomed to the darkness, John could perceive the dim outline of a man who carried a gun over his shoulder.

" Can't you shoot ? " " Varmer John" called out.

" Aye, but I'm aveard I shall miss'n. Do 'ee come quick zur. 'Tis master's gun an' 'ee told I t' come an' ask 'ee to shoot 'n."

Thinking further delay dangerous, John flung on his clothes, ran downstairs and took the gun from the agitated man, who still stood gazing at the window, as if from thence would come his aid.

" Now, then, where is the animal ? " commanded " Varmer John," now fully awake, a sense of danger quickening his senses. But even as he spoke he heard a frenzied bark and the creature came careering madly towards them.

" Stand still, man ! "

The dog tore past them and steadily John took aim ; there was a sharp report and then silence. They walked a few yards down the winding lane, outside the house, and there by the side of the road lay the poor creature, its wild suffering over. The bullet had struck its head, it lay with its tongue out, its last desire being, no doubt, to slake its terrible thirst at the river, which lay just beyond the bend in the lane.

" He's dead, zur, dead's a door nail," said the man.

" Isn't that what you wanted ? " enquired John.

" Yes, zur, but he were a beautiful creature avore this madness took 'n, would'n 'urt man, woman nor child. He were the best-natured dog around about yer. But thank 'ee, zur," he added with a sniff, " You be a game young feller, I don't wonder the maidens be after 'ee. Will 'ee promise, zur, that you won't zay nothin' about this yer business ? "

" Why, yes, if you wish it," grinned " Varmer John."

" Thank 'ee, zur. I'm much obliged to 'ee. Now I can tell maister 'twere I as shot 'n, an' perhaps he'll raise me wages."

THE COUNTRYMAN SCORES

Standing outside a certain wayside inn, in the heart of the country, I noted what should have been a young man to whom life was an adventure. He had taken up his stand there for the want of something better to do, waiting no doubt for some of his fellows to join him in contemplation of nothing in particular.

He looked less intelligent and less animated than the cows in the nearby field . . . . One aspect of Country Life.

In London recently I watched the sallow-faced hurrying crowds in the racket of modern life, absorbed mostly in their business and their newspapers, sparing perhaps a glance for a shapely ankle or a pretty face . . . . Town Life ?

Neither of them a fair criterion, but each in its way superficially true.

The best type of countryman, however, is steady and philosophic, possessing a wisdom that comes of studying the face of the earth and the whims of men and animals. He is not obsessed with the thought, "I must get away." His work is his life and unversed in the teaching of Plato or Socrates he yet is wise in the contemplation of his universe. He has no problem but the weather for he knows that toil must bring its reward and the seasons their harvest. He has accepted life and has thereby gained a sort of contentment that knows nothing of idleness.

Living close to nature he is seldom known to possess the town-dwellers craving for excitement. He has found, as it were, an answer that every human being seeks at one time or another, to the riddle of his own existence.

He beholds with satisfaction the three-fold creation of animals, crops and the fruit of his own body. The result of his handiwork in co-operation with the forces of nature is everywhere about him. Life at times may be hard but it is nevertheless just and patience must win in the end.

On the other hand the 'man about town' is alert and practical, ever conscious of being a cog in the wheel of progress.

Life, to most in the city, is a battle of wits and a giving out of energy towards a scheme in which each individual plays but a small part. Their wits are sharpened but their senses dulled in the ever-increasing demand upon their resources. Caught up in the stream of life they have neither time nor inclination for meditation but take their 'ready-made' pleasures as part of the day's routine.

In the business of seeking a livelihood they have missed the art of living, at least, so it would appear to the country-mind.

But the town-born loves the rush and tear and noise ; he is so accustomed to the scheduled existence and 'canned' pleasures that he turns with contempt upon the country-bred, for does not the world, in his estimation, revolve around Trafalgar Square ?

So what would you ?

It's a question of mentality. The town-dweller does not seek to alter the mode of his existence provided he is sufficently paid. This, however, does not alter the fact that a return to the old craftsmanship and pride in the finished article would be more soul-satisfying to these victims of mass-production.

Unconscious of their need they rush through their days, filling their leisure hours in occupations which lack the stamp of individuality and shortening their hours of sleep to grasp at new sensations.

The farm-labourer may have been underpaid in coin, but life has more to offer him in terms of sunshine and fresh air than to the struggling ledger-clerk tied to the office stool.

The flaws are there, both in Town and Country Life, but surely the countryman more nearly reaches the standard attained in that ideal state described by some dreaming philosopher :—

> " Where no man shall work for money,
> And no man shall work for fame
> But all for the love of working."

THE VILLAGE OF HINTON ST. MARY

HINTON ST. MARY is a typically unspoilt English Village, Church, Manor, Village Inn, farmsteads and thatched cottages form the traditional picture of rural England. Even the wayside pond, opposite the inn, complete with ducks and moor-hens add one more touch to this rustic scene of peace and tranquility.

The Village Church, dedicated in the first instance to St. Peter, was originally The Chapel of the Ecclesiastical Manor which belonged to The Shaston Abbey of St. Mary in the reign of Henry VIII. The square tower is early 15th century Gothic on the foundations of an even earlier one.

In 1863 the parish was made a perpetual curacy and became a vicarage and The Vicar of Iwerne, to which minster the church is attached, acquired its patronage.

The first vicar of Hinton St. Mary Church was the Rev. Charles Nicol, M.A. of Worcester College, Oxford. An annual parish festival, held in commemoration of the original dedication of the Church, was held on St. Peter's day, June 29th, but eventually this was discontinued and the vigil degenerated into a fair or market.

In Doomsday Book, Hinton is spelt Haintone. The derivation being from ' hind ' (hand) and ' ton ' (town), that is, the village was originally a lay-brothers' settlement appropriated to ' hand ' labour. The Church, having been later dedicated to St. Mary on account of its former association with the Shaston Abbey of that name, the village now became known as Hinton St. Mary.

Standing within the grounds of The Manor House is The Old Tithe Barn, now The Manor Theatre. This tithe barn, like most of those which have survived, was built in the XIIIth century and is a fine example of early English architecture.

The Old Tithe Hinton Barn has been for many generations the centre of the social activities of the village and has become inseparable from the name of Hinton St. Mary.

Originally before the Reformation the barn was used to store the produce of The Abbey farms. These farms, which were attached to The Manor, were often tilled by monks, or, as in the case of Hinton, by lay-brothers.

In addition to this, the tithes of corn and of kind exacted from the parishioners and the Abbey tenants together with rents in kind were stored in the old Tithe Barn.

In the reign of Henry VIII the Manor was granted to William Sturton, afterwards 7th Lord Stourton, from a Wiltshire family of great antiquity.

In Richard II's reign John de Stourton had been Sheriff for the Counties of Somerset and Dorset, and, in the reign of Mary, his descendant Charles, the 8th Lord Stourton, was appointed Lord Lieutenant of Wiltshire, Somerset and Dorset.

This nobleman, however, died seised of his manors, amongst which was that of Hinton St. Mary which was granted to one Robert Freke, a teller of the Exchequer and father of Sir Thomas Freke, M.P., and his heirs and was inherited by the Pitts of Stratfield-Say.

This same nobleman, once of Hinton Manor, was long remembered as "the Wicked Nobleman", on account of his having been convicted, together with four of his servants, for the murder of William Hartgill, who had been his father's steward.

He was executed at Salisbury, on March 16th, 1556, and according to the privilege of his rank, was hanged with a halter of silk. Legend has it that the condemned nobleman, hoping for reprieve, sent the Queen a ring she had at one time given him, but the appeal was in vain.

Thomas Freke, son of Sir Thomas Freke of Shroton, reconstructed the Manor House in the early XVIIth century and later in 1664 a new wing was added. The family arms are carved over the front door and the Church contains a monument at the North wall to this Thomas Freke.

Mary Freke, his widow, left a somewhat unusual bequest to the effect that the Vicar of the parish should hear the children diligently in the Catechism and that two worthy widows or elderly spinsters and two apprentices of the parish should receive succout. This bequest is still paid annually and the benefits apportioned to these objects.

It was in the sixth year of the reign of Elizabeth I that the Manor of Hinton St. Mary was granted to Robert Freke who had previously purchased Shroton Manor from Lord Pembroke, and seven successive members of his family were tenants of the Manor House at Hinton St. Mary. From 1698 they were tenants under the Pitts, afterwards the Lords Rivers of Rushmore and Stratfield-Say.

The Pitts of Stratfield-Say and the present Lord of the Manor are in the direct line of descent from Sir William Pitt, Comptroller of the Household and Principal Officer of the Exchequer in the reigns of Elizabeth I, James I and Charles I ; who was granted the manors of Sturminster Newton and Bagber by Elizabeth.

It was from Thomas, younger brother of Sir William Pitt, settled at Blandford St. Mary that William Pitt, Earl of Chatham, was descended, and his second son known as William Pitt the Younger.

To-day the monastic beauty of the interior of the Manor is enriched by a selection of some of the finest pictures in the world, some, in fact, are unique, for the present Lord of the Manor, besides being a noted anthropologist is a connoisseur of art. The walls are adorned, not only with magnificent paintings, but framed embroideries of great delicacy and beauty. In a small alcove on one of the landings is a fresco from the temples of Ancient Greece.

The atmosphere of the Manor, produced from exquisite taste is one of subdued splendour and satisfying beauty. The house is perfectly appointed so that the harmony produced is as unbroken as that of a Beethoven Symphony.

Nature alone could rival this acquisition of beauty and it would seem that, knowing this, she has, with ten-fold prodigality, flung out before the gates of this Manor House the glorious panorama of the Blackmore Vale.

The Manor and Tithe Barn is, by kind permission of the Lord of The Manor, occasionally open to the public, the proceeds derived therefrom being apportioned to the building of a Town Hall in Sturminster Newton, which is part of his estate.

One might say of this village of Hinton St. Mary, so rich in tradition and ancestral pride, that ' here is some corner', not of a ' foreign field ', but of our smiling countryside, 'which is forever England '.

NOTE. I am indebted to Mr. Pitt-Rivers for supplying and checking notes of the Ancient Manors of Sturminster Newton and Hinton St. Mary.

THE OLD RECTORY, HAMWORTHY

POOLE

THE OLD RECTORY OF HAMWORTHY, a three-storied Jacobean building stands, rich in historical associations, and in striking contrast to its neighbour, the Herbert Carter Secondary Modern School.

This early Jacobean house, hidden from view by surrounding trees, contains much of great interest to those who care to delve into its past.

The beautifully carved old fireplace with its ingle-nook and worn curb, the oaken beams, the hooks for curing hams suspended from the roof of what was once the kitchen, the powder-closet adjoining one of the spacious bedrooms, the wide and imposing staircase, all bespeak a former dignity of this sometime manor in the village of Hamworthy.

The house was originally built as a manor between the years 1600 and 1610 and became the seat of the old family of Carew.

In Cromwell's time the property was sequestrated owing to the fact that the family gave its support to the Royalists during the Civil War. It thus came about that the old rectory claims the distinction of having housed Cromwell himself, and the wounded of his band of Ironsides who stormed the fortress of Corfe Castle in 1643. The top storey then was all one room and here the injured were brought and those who died were buried, so they say, in the churchyard nearby.

The inhabitants of Hamworthy will point out now, a lonely mound without headstones or cross which, they say, marks the spot where these followers of Cromwell lay, and up to within a few years of the present time the top room of the old rectory was still called the ' hospital '.

There are in evidence in one of the outside walls several bricked-up windows. This was apparently a ruse to avoid the Window Tax in 1697, during the reign of William III upon " houses graduated according to number of windows over six ".

It was, however, after the Restoration, when the property again came into the possession of the Carews that romance, intrigue and passion followed in its train.

The lady of the manor, it was said, was enamoured of her cousin, the handsome, "devil-may-care Carew" around whom legendary stories had grown up.

This same Carew apparently had great skill and power in the taming of animals. He was reputed to have appeared clad in an animal's skin, imitating the cry and habits of the creature he represented in a convincingly realistic manner.

He could reproduce the call of a bird or the cry of an

animal to the extent that his best friends (or enemies) were deceived.

A wild story was told of Devil-may-Care Carew that he once killed a man, skinned him and donned the skin himself with, no doubt, the freakish idea of impersonating the man he had murdered.

The unholy spell he possessed was cast upon the lovely lady of the manor, then married to his cousin bearing his name.

For long this wild and unscrupulous lover came at night to lure away his cousin's wife, using as his love-call the vibrant whistle of a bird.

But eventually the Lord of the Manor discovered their secret and going out one evening found them in each other's arms. He shot them both. Disposing of the body of Carew in the pond which was close to the manor, he carried that of his wife inside.

Thus the tragedy—and still, so the story goes, may be heard on quiet evenings, the low whistle of the wild Devil-may-Care Carew for his stolen love.

During the Napoleonic Wars the old rectory again figures in history as having been the Headquarters of the Southern Command and when the Duke of Wellington came to review the troops he is said to have stayed in this building.

Apparently the officers were billetted in the larger houses and the men in the smaller, hence the name ' Battery Cottages' was given to the more humble dwellings near the bridge.

Then again, at the back of the house, there is said to be an underground tunnel running to the harbour, used, no doubt, by smugglers. This, of course, is quite a possibility as smuggling was, at this time, rife in the district owing to its easy landing places, sandy coves and natural caves.

Thus then has the old rectory of Hamworthy played a distinct part in the high lights of history.

It is now falling into disrepair, its exterior, however, still retains its simple dignity and beauty of line and promises if undisturbed, to weather many a year to come, before it eventually crumbles to the dust and its ghost is well and truly laid.

PLUMBER MANOR

PLUMBER MANOR, situated about three miles from Sturminster Newton, has been in the possession of the Brunes from early in the seventeenth century till the present day. It was rebuilt and enlarged by Charles P. Brune of Place House, Cornwall, to whom it belonged in 1871.

This imposing Jacobean structure, built from local stone, stands well back on its extensive lawns, dotted with fine old trees. Besides being another of our Wessex monuments it has a charm which is all its own.

The original Manor is mentioned in Domesday Book where it is stated that "Swain, one of the King's thanes, holds Plumbere, and Ralph of him. His father held it in King Edward's time and it was taxed for five hides (120 acres).

There is one land to three ploughs, there is one plough in the demesne and five borders and three villeins and six borders with one plough. There are sixteen acres of meadow, wood five quarentens (furlongs) long and three quarentens broad. It was worth thirty shillings, now sixty shillings (1806)."

Domesday Book also gives an interesting aside concerning

the lay-out of the Plumber estate. It says " Uluric the huntsman holds one hide of the King William I. His father held it in King Edward's time and it was taxed for as much so much. There is land to one plough. There are three borders there and three acres of meadow. It is worth 10/-."

'Uluric the huntsman' suggests that here in the Forest of Blackmore where he held one hide (24 acres) of the Plumber Estate, was the scene of much hunting of the deer. It was in fact for many years the favourite hunting ground of kings.

In Caesar's time this fertile vale must have been singled out for sport for legend says that Caesar commanded a ring to be placed around a stag's neck in this vicinity in order to spare its life.

Later Henry III is reputed to have hunted here a beautiful white hart but spared its life. When later it was killed by one Thomas de la Lynd the county was forced to pay a permanent fine called " White Hart Silver ".

All this, of course, points to the fact that the Manor was originally Saxon and flourished under the rule of its feudal Lord somewhere in the days before the Norman Conquest and afterwards under Norman rule.

The Brune family, now Prideaux-Brune, is of Norman descent. The family vault, under the square mausoleum, is to be found on the north side of the churchyard at Fifehead Neville, the neighbouring parish.

One's first impression on entering the Manor now, is that the ghost, so long reputed to haunt this house, must have been most well and truly laid, for anything less likely to harbour some tormented dweller of the tombs is difficult to imagine. The house looks lived in and delightful, and no hint of past tragedy hangs in the air.

A painting of the Manor as it was when first built hangs over the stair-case in the hall. It was a three-eyed building surrounded on all sides by stone walls. A few relics of the latter may still be found at the back of the house.

The minstrel-gallery is part of the original building, and

at one time was the vantage point for viewing unobserved the festive gaiety in the room below. It is now a pleasant apartment on the walls of which hang the family portraits.

Adjoining the gallery is the Haunted Room and it was from this room that the ghost of a some-time Lord of the Manor, clad only in night attire, was supposed to have rushed madly through the gallery and down the stairs. This apparition always coincided with the baying of the hounds which could be distinctly heard at the back of the house, and it was this echo which the visitant pursued.

The story goes that long ago one of the Lords of Plumber Manor was torn to pieces by his hounds. Early one morning they had started a fight among themselves and the noise of their fierce baying had awakened their master.

Without stopping to dress he had rushed from his bedroom, through the gallery to his hounds at the back of the house where the fight was raging.

Gallantly he attempted to separate the infuriated animals with the result that they turned on him and tore him to pieces and, according to the local account of the incident, only two thumbs were left of the unfortunate and much-respected Lord of the Manor.

For long this precipitant ghost was said to haunt the premises but now the baying of the hounds is never heard nor the agitated spectre ever seen.

There is a particularly interesting room leading from the hall on the ground floor containing a large fireplace which, at one time, harboured four bread-ovens. The walls are adorned with interesting childhood studies of the Brune family by Opie, the Cornish artist.

One or two of the original fireplaces are to be found in some of the rooms and the front door boasts the original heavy brass knocker.

Directly in front of the house there is a very attractive and well-built stone bridge over a winding stream. It has three arches in Early English style.

The path over this bridge to the front door was the original entrance to the Manor. Now this is disused and the houses approached by a wide gateway to the left of the rustic bridge.

In a corner of a field close to the Manor is what had been called by many generations the Petrifying Spring. This spring is dangerous to children as it somehow forms a swirl of mud which produces a kind of suction capable of drowning a child.

To-day, however, all precautions have been made so that such a thing could never take palce and the Petrifying Spring is no more to be feared than the Manor Ghost.

RACEDOWN

I HAVE BEFORE ME two delicately-tinted roses picked by Lady Pinney's own hand from her garden at Racedown and given to me as a memento of my visit to her beautiful home on the borders of Dorset and Devon.

These roses are a symbol of the living memories which crowd this Georgian house and are so much part of the place. So true is this that Lady Pinney told me that one September night, having sat up late, half-dozing in her chair, she was awakened by confused noises which might have been the sound of carriage-wheels and the knocking of the front door. In that state between waking and sleeping, it seemed to Lady Pinney that it was the arrival of " Mr. and Miss Wordsworth " at the midnight hour, for so, actually, did these visitors arrive at Racedown on a September night in 1795.

It was a conclusion of a Radio Programme which Lady Pinney heard, but, steeped in her knowledge of incidents concerning the poet Wordsworth and his sister Dorothy whilst at Racedown, it seemed to her at that moment that the past had returned once more.

Lady Pinney has in her possession a unique collection of letters, account-books and receipts which concerns the private lives of the Wordsworths whilst at Racedown. These papers were unearthed in the eighteen-fifties by a niece of the youngest son of John Pinney who in 1831 was Mayor of Bristol.

For two generations, however, these papers were forgotten. It was not until Lady Pinney and her husband, Major-General Sir Reginald Pinney came to live at Racedown that the former, by extensive research, allied to her vivid sense of imagination, has brought to life, not only the poet's stay in Dorset, but the history of the Pinney Family who were instrumental in bringing the Wordsworths to Racedown.

We know now that the Pinneys can be traced back to the early fifteenth century, but that John Pinney the Puritan Preacher is " the first of his line to stand out as a personality" and the first to leave any record of his career.

Three of the descendants from the Puritan's large family made their mark in history : Hester, who never married, is remembered as having made lace and sold it on the Royal Exchange ; Azariah, who took part in the Monmouth Rebellion and was thereby first gaoled at Dorchester and then transported to the West Indies ; and Nathaniel, who stayed at home, married an heiress and with the commercial faculty of the other two, carrried on a successful business at Bristol and Bettiscombe. Azariah, who had amassed great wealth in the Indies, at length returned to Bettiscombe and became High Sheriff of Dorset. Nathaniel's son, Azariah, was joined here by his cousin, John Frederick Pinney, grandson of the Monmouth rebel and the two cousins, who lived in great style, were often seen driving in state through the roads at Broadwindsor in a heavy coach drawn by six horses.

It was John Frederick Pinney who planned and built Racedown in the middle of the eighteenth century. He lived here for a short while with his cousin Azariah, but they died within two years of each other and were buried side by side in Wayford Church.

Now the family fortune was inherited by one John Pretor,

a cousin, who assumed the surname of Pinney. He improved Racedown Lodge and handed it over to his eldest son John Frederick.

It was this John Frederick Pinney who became a close friend of William Wordsworth and it was he who invited the poet and his sister Dorothy to live rent-free at Racedown in September, 1795.

Here they lived till July, 1797 in the seclusion of this country home, within sight of the sea and the lovely wooded hills of West Dorset. Dorothy later described it as " the place dearest to my recollection on the whole surface of the Island ".*

The poet and his sister were very fond of walking and the latter describes this part of the county in her letters written during her stay at Racedown. She praises, in particular, the hills, as they remind her of her " native wilds ". She pronounces their greatest inconvenience the distance from the Post Office, but says that this is overcome as her brother " is so good a walker ".

Here Wordsworth wrote the two poems " The Borderers " and " Guilt and Sorrow ".

The heavy sadness of the latter poem is no doubt accounted for by the poet's recent unhappy love-affair in France. Wordsworth was not by nature a profligate and it grieved him to know that he could not legalise the affair with the woman he obviously loved.

The Wordsworths' means were limited. They had, in fact, to subsist upon £70 to £80 a year. In some of their letters there is reference made to their ' coursing ' or hunting the hare. This they seem to have done a great deal of, no doubt to replenish their rather scanty larder. Mention is made that the pitiable expression of the dying animal did not, however, deter Wordsworth from enjoying a good meal of its flesh !

---

* A History of Broadwindsor. (Taylor Milne.)

The Wordsworths entertained many friends at Racedown, among whom were Mary Hutchinson, who became the poet's wife, Basil Montague, the legal writer and James Tobin, the dramatist.

It is recounted in a copy of one of the letters that " One June day a tall, pale-faced young man leapt over the gate into the meadow and ran down to the house ". It was Samuel Taylor Coleridge.

Coleridge had previously met Wordsworth at the Pinney's house in Bristol. Now he met Dorothy and the three formed a perfect trio and entered into deep discussions at Racedown. Dorothy, although somewhat shy and retiring by nature, nevertheless possessed great personality and charm. She undoubtedly influenced the writing of these two great men for the " Lyrical Ballads " were inspired by these discussions.

In the Summer of 1797, Wordsworth and his sister were invited to join Coleridge at Nether Stowey and so they left Racedown, to which they owed so much.

Here they had lived in peace and tranquility for close on two years. Here midst the beauty of the Dorset hills and dales, Wordsworth found expression for his deep sorrow and grew so close to Nature that he developed a philosophy which made him a poet for all time.

Dorset people will be ever proud to know that this countryside helped to inspire one of the greatest of Nature's poets.

" Say something to me in Dorset," said Lady Pinney. " I'm a cockney and can't talk the dialect."

" This is where thick poet used t'bide," were the words which came to my lips, " an' 'twas Dosset vlowers did help t'make'n zing."

KINGSTON LACY

KINGSTON LACY, like many more stately homes is now, on certain days, open to the public. This place which is so much a part of Dorset is a gem of artistic and historical interest.

The manor of Kingston Lacy, situated about two miles north-west of Wimborne, originally belonged to the de Lacy family. It then passed into Royal hands and was later granted by James I to one Charles Blount.

It was from his son, Mountjoy, Earl of Newport, that Sir John Bankes, Chief Justice of the Common Pleas, purchased the estate. He was a Royalist, but of moderate views, so was allowed to remain in office by Parliament.

A few years before the outbreak of the Civil War Sir John purchased Corfe Castle and established his family there whilst he himself was detained in attendance upon the King, Charles I, both at York and at Oxford. It was at Oxford that Sir John died in 1644 and was buried in Christ Church Cathedral.

During the absence of her husband, Lady Bankes held the fortress of Corfe Castle over a period of three years, against the Parliamentary forces. After the demolition of the Castle, on account of her bravery, Lady Bankes was allowed to retain the Keys, which still remain in the possession of the Bankes' family.

At the Restoration, Sir Ralph Bankes, then the head of the family, decided to build a new country house at Kingston Lacy.

He chose for the site a spot, on which according to tradition, had stood a palace of the West Saxon Kings, close to the ancient hill fortress of Badbury Rings.

So in the year 1660, Kingston Lacy House was built to designs by Sir Roger Pratt, who was held in high esteem and was, with Wren, commissioned for the rebuilding of London after the Great Fire.

Early in the nineteenth century the Lord of the Manor was Mr. William John Bankes who was an art connoisseur of note. He was a friend of Lord Byron and during the Peninsular War was aide-de-camp to the Duke of Wellington.

Mr. William Bankes acquired a fine collection of Spanish paintings and these adorn the walls of the Spanish Room of the interior of the house. This is a strikingly beautiful room. Every painting is Spanish with the exception of the ceiling which was designed by Sansovino and came from the Contarini Palace in Venice.

Between the years 1835 and 1839 many alterations were carried out by the architect Sir Charles Barry. He covered the original brickwork of the house by grey stone, and re-introduced the roof platform and cupola to which Sir Roger Pratt had attached so much importance. He also lowered the ground in front of the house and made the entrance direct into the ground floor. Originally the chief floor of the house was on a mezzanine floor, after the style of Italian palaces, which was reached by a sweeping staircase on the outside.

Barry, after having made the ground-floor entrance, now added the magnificent marble staircase which leads to the principal floor, also the dormers, chimney-stacks and the attic feature in the centre of the South front.

The marble staircase is perhaps the most impressive feature of the whole erection. In the process of building the measurement of each stair was sent to Italy and as each was completed it was shipped to Poole and erected, piece by piece. The variegated marbles used for the balustrades stand out in marked contrast to the white marble of the stairs.

The view from the half-landing of the sunken garden and the park beyond is both restful and beautiful.

The three bronze statues by Baron Marochetti of Sir John and Lady Bankes (the latter holding a sword and the key of Corfe Castel), and King Charles I, stand in niches on the landing, and like the balustrades, are in sharp contrast to the marble.

The library is an imposing room, containing above the books, family portraits and notable pictures, many of which were painted by Sir Peter Lely—the Court painter of the day, who stayed in the house whilst at work on the portraits.

Reynolds, accompanied by Dr. Johnson, visited the house and was said to have remarked, " I never had appreciated Sir Peter Lely till I had seen these portraits ".

Johnson, according to Boswell, in his habitual eccentric manner, appeared to take no interest in the masterpieces around him but retired to a corner where he began ' stretching out his right leg as far as he could before him, then bringing up his left leg, and stretching his right leg further on ". Mr. Bankes is reputed, on account of Johnson's queer behaviour, to have informed him that although the house was old the flooring was perfectly safe. At which, Boswell says, the Doctor " started from his reverie like a person wakened out of his sleep, but spake not a word ".

The Drawing Room, in French style of the Louis XV period, contains family portraits by Romney, Van Dyck, Sir Joshua Reynolds and Weigall. Another interesting feature of this room is a unique collection of Enamels by Henry Bone of Queen Elizabeth and her Court.

The Dining Room, panelled in oak and cedar, is particularly imposing. The carved doors are of Italian box-wood, the execution of which is extremely beautiful and took four years to complete. A Gobelin tapestry, which was awarded First Prize at an Exhibition held at Windsor, adorns one of the walls, and four panels painted on canvas by Annabale Carracci. Other notable pictures in this room include an unfinished painting by Giorgione.

The Saloon is the most impressive of all the ground-floor rooms. It is two storeys in height and has a ceiling of great beauty, painted by Italian artists.

The panels of the doors leading from this room into the Drawing Room are from the Hall of the Vatican and were designed for Pope Pius III.

There is an inlaid ivory and ebony cabinet in Goa work which was made by a colony of Portuguese settlers in India, possibly followers of Vasco da Gama. Standing near this cabinet is a carving of the Last Supper by Hans Mayr, who was for many years the Christ in the Passion Play at Oberammergau.

Here, as in the other rooms, are many pictures of outstanding character and celebrity, one of particular interest being that by Rubens of the Marchesa Brignole Spinola in her wedding dress. The Marchesa has a vivid beauty and Rubens is reputed to have been greatly enamoured of her.

The grounds in front of the house are particularly lovely and distinguished visitors have marked the occasion of their stay here in such a way that for many generations it will be a living memory. The late Queen Mary, when Princess of Wales, planted the liquid amber on the lawn and King Edward VII one of the cedars. The Duke of Wellington chose the site and laid the foundation stone of the obelisk which was brought from the Island of Philae to the Manor of Kingston Lacy. He also planted the cedar of Lebanon on the lawn.

Dorset may be justly proud to number this beautiful and dignified ancestral mansion among her country seats.

WOOLBRIDGE MANOR

WOOLBRIDGE MANOR HOUSE standing on the banks of the Dorset Frome and in close proximity to the ancient bridge which supplies part of its name, is a Jacobean building of great dignity and charm.

Although in its own right this Manor is one of the most picturesque in the county, it is its association with Hardy's "Tess of the D'Urbervilles" which has made it the best known, for it was to this house that Angel Clare brought his bride on their ill-fated wedding night.

Woolbridge Manor was at one time the seat of the Turberville family, their principal residence being at Bere Regis. Hardy slightly alters the names of people and places but it is obvious that he writes of the Turberville family, making Tess a humble descendant.

The Turbervilles were established at Bere Regis in the reign of Edward II, but nothing now of their Manor remains.

In the reign of Queen Elizabeth I a younger son, Thomas Turberville, owned Woolbridge Manor, which had been before the dissolution of the Monasteries part of Bindon Abbey.

It was the son of Thomas Turberville who succeeded both to the Woolbridge and Bere estates which remained in the family until the male line became extinct.

The last of the Turbervilles left twin daughters as his heirs. These two died on the same day at the same house at the age of twenty-seven.

The Manor House composed of brick, tile and stone now mellowed with age, is still further beautified by moss and lichen on roof and gables.

It was built in the twelfth century and restored in the seventeenth. The house is said to have been garrisoned during the Civil War whilst it was owned by Sir John Turberville, at that time Sheriff of the County. It is possible that the building was damaged at this time and restored at the date given on the stone over the porch (1653).

The main front, which faces North, is seventeenth-century brickwork whilst the gables at either end are probably much older. The bricked chimneys containing pairs of arched niches which are so much a feature of this Manor, are also probably seventeenth century.

According to Hutchins the Turberville Arms, impaling Howard of Bindon, were, in his day to be seen over a door in the hall.

These, however, have gone but there still remain the partially obliterated portraits of the two Turberville ladies built into the walls on the upstairs landing. It was these paintings which Tess found so disturbing on her wedding night.

Originally the Manor and Chapel Barn were part of the monastery of Bindon Abbey when the monks exacted toll from the bridge.

The North wall of the Chapel Barn is probably a remnant of the original Saxon building for a part of the old herringbone masonry is still visible. This indicates that the barn is older than either the Manor or Bindon Abbey and in common with many another Saxon Chapel was built on a bridge to further the interests of an ancient monastery.

There is said to be an underground tunnel from Woolbridge Manor to Bindon Abbey which runs under the river. This was no doubt used as a means of escape in times of religious persecution.

Like most of these ancient Manors, Woolbridge is said to harbour a ghost connected with some former Lord of the Manor. In this case a bygone Turberville is supposed to have committed a felonious crime in the family coach. Since that time the coach and four is reputed to have been seen driving out in the gloom of the evening from Woolbridge House. It may only, however, be seen by those of Turberville blood.

There is a story told that a certain gentleman, when on his way one evening to dine with friends, saw a queer old-fashioned four-in-hand drive over the bridge accompanied by outriders. The gentleman, puzzled by this spectacle, made enquiries as to whether any one in the district owned such an equipage. He was told that no one owned a vehicle of that description but that he had without doubt seen the Turberville Coach. It is unnecessary to add that the man had the Turberville blood in his veins.

Hardy brings a hint of the same superstition into his story of Tess, for the latter makes the remark that she seems to have seen before the old-fashioned post-chaise which was to take her and Angel Clare on their honeymoon.

This vague reference reminds Clare of the 'ghostly appearance of the Turberville Coach' and he tells Tess the story. With a strange foreboding Tess asks : "Do we see it when we are going to die or when we have committed a crime ?" To this Clare makes no reply and Tess carries in her heart the lurking premonition of sorrow and tragedy to come.

It was at the Woolbridge Manor House that Tess, on the evening of her wedding day, made the confession to her husband which caused an estrangement so deep, that, to Angel Clare, Tess was dead.

With this deep conviction in his sub-conscious mind, Clare, who under great stress of emotion was given to sleep-walking, carried Tess in his sleep and laid her in an empty stone coffin in the ruins at Bindon Abbey.

It is a tribute to the genius of Hardy that Tess is real to Dorset folk to-day and it is not, therefore, surprising to learn that not long ago one of the maids at Woolbridge Manor House, steeped no doubt in the pathetic story of the ill-fated honeymoon, remarked to her mistress that she had seen Tess come from her bedroom clad in her nightdress, her dark hair falling below her waist.

STURMINSTER NEWTON IN THE OLD DAYS

STURMINSTER NEWTON, like many another Market Town, has changed considerably during the last seventy odd years. The place has grown almost to twice its former size, at the same time losing much of its character and individuality, owing no doubt to the predominance of mechanism and mass production.

I am indebted to my father for this picture of my native town so long ago, which he has handed down to me—Sturminster Newton as he saw it when a boy.

In those days the market was very flourishing, indeed, it was said to be one of the largest in the whole of the south of England.

The old preaching Cross, which still stands, was then used as a means of displaying cheeses, butter, eggs and vegetables. These were arranged on and around the steps of the cross whilst the salesmen cried their wares from the vantage point of the erection.

The 'Market Place' was then the centre of the whole market.

Pigs, cows, sheep and dairy produce were bought and sold under the eye of all and sundry, midst hearty greetings, and back chat, a jovial gathering of folks from miles around all clad in their 'second best'.

The 'pig market' extended from what is now the Masonic Hall to Messrs. Barnett's ironmonger's shop, a series of pens and places allotted to hundreds of pigs sold, not by auction, but by barter.

Then, from the National Provincial Bank extending around the whole of the market place, leaving, of course, openings for entering the various shops, were posts and railings tied to which were hundreds of cows and calves all to be sold on the same lines as the pigs, *i.e.*, on the judgment of the prospective buyer. Here then, was an occasion for much country humour and witticism, both buyer and seller displaying a shrewdness, somewhat belied by their slow and non-committal appearance.

From Messrs. Senior & Godwin's offices into White Lane (now Bath Road) was the Sheep Market. This apparently like the tired creatures here for sale, produced less merriment and back chat than the sale of the stalwart beasts to left and right.

From the Police Station corner to the front of Messrs. Strange's shop were ranged horse and ponies for sale.

Thus then was the market square a lively hum of bartering and selling and jovial gossip, on the fortnightly market, second to none in the south of England.

Here, too, was held the annual Fair, an old custom dating back to Medieval times, where most of the local trade was done.

There was no Coronation Lamp in the Market Place in those days so that there was ample space for rows of Standings displaying their fairings, sweets, 'brandy-balls,' cakes and toys, and for the side-shows exhibiting 'The Fat Woman', 'The Black Man', 'Boxer', 'The Dwarf', and such like rare specimens of humanity.

Sturminster Fair was a big occasion. The local schools were closed and people came from miles around to celebrate the event.

Beer was strong and plentiful and produced the fighting spirit. Never a fair was held without a fight adding to the general entertainment. Even at Club Walks or Christmas Band Playing these fights occurred on the smallest provocation.

A sight my father witnessed on such a fair day as this redolent of the days of Street Ballads, was that of a tall blind man, playing a concertina. He was led by a strapping girl, his walking stick stuck in his buttonhole.

This man sang as he played, songs which he afterwards sold at a penny each. Some were for the farmer and some for the workers. They each reflected the spirit of the times.

The song for the farmer was against taxation and ran as follows :

"They are going to tax the butter,
They are going to tax the cheese,
They are going to tax old women's teeth,
They'll tax the bugs and fleas."

That for the labourer had a rousing chorus :

"Strike, boys, strike for better wages,
Stand out as long as you can get a meal,
The farming men say
You will surely win the day,
If you only put your shoulder to the wheel."

So much for Sturminster Fair. Now I turn to the crafts and trades then pursued by the inhabitants of an old town.

Near the church facing the river Stour was a Tan Yard. The house standing there to-day is still called Tan Yard Farm. My father could remember the large sheds on high poles for storing the oak bark and the pits close by for soaking the skins.

The owner of the Tan Yard in my grandfather's time was a man called Isaacs, who was a Quaker.

My grandfather, when a boy, visited the home of Mr. Isaacs and when asked in the good old Dorset way if he would have something to eat, he replied, " No, thank you."

On being asked a little later he said he would.

" No, you won't," replied Mr. Isaacs, "you are not going tell lies in my house."

Leaving the Tan Yard and coming up the hill from the Boys' School you arrive at the house on the left-hand side which once belonged to Mr. John Pope, the cooper.

His business was flourishing as he was an expert at the craft. In my father's own words, " I can now see him in my mind with a hammer and another tool walking around a large barrel during down the hoops. As he went round, between every hit he used to throw out his 'game' leg and foot, bump, flop ; bump, flop, until the hoop was in its place. Cooper Pope always had work. He had a daughter Lavinia."

There was no back door or yard to this rather strange looking house and for this reason Cooper Pope had to stable his pony in a shed at the front.

One summer day, when the pony was out 'to grass' some Russians called with two Polar bears which had been performing through the streets. They were allowed to sleep, both man and bears in the pony's shed.

Again in my father's words : " I can see those bears and hear the dull voices of the men saying :

" Arum barum, bum bum bardee.
Arum, barum, bum, bum, bee."

This they kept repeating holding the bears with a long chain each and helping them to go round with the aid of a long pole, occasionally throwing the pole to the bear who caught it and passed it back to the master."

Pit-sawing by hand was another trade which flourished in those days. There were saw-pits in every timber merchant's and carpenter's yard of any importance. They are now all filled up and sawing is done by machinery in the big saw mills.

Another occupation was that of horse-training. This, of course, is now reduced to a minimum since the introduction of cars, buses, motor-bicycles, etc.

My father could remember Mr. George Dowling and his helpers at their work, burning all the hair from the horses (singeing, it was called).

A much rarer sight than of old is the blacksmith at his forge. No longer now do the children from the Old Wesleyan Day School pause on their way from school to watch the sparks fly from the anvil or the flames leap in the smithy that stood facing Church Street for so many years.

Other crafts carried on in Sturminster Newton at this time were weaving, button-making, rush-basket making (from the withey beds in the river), rope-making and brush-making. All are now extinct.

Amidst all these changes, however, there are those things which have remained little changed throughout the years. One of these is the view from Newstock Hill at the Vale of Blackmore. Once more I will use my father's own words about this view through an old man's eyes :

"At the top of Tewstock Hill, facing east, south and west, you can see a landscape second to none anywhere in England.

" In the east, the River Stour, like a silver serpent glides along, and overshadowing the rivers and fields you can see the Dorset Heights, Iwerne, Shroton, Stourpaine Hills looking as if on guard to protect all and sundry within the Vale.

" Now, turn south and find a grand and beautiful wood, called Piddles Wood, still backed up by our ancient Dorset Hills, which seems to be ever a beauty and joy for those who have eyes to see.

" Then turning to the right and facing west you can see the Vale of Blackmore in all its glory. How I wish I could command words to describe its peace, prosperity, beauty. The River Stour can clearly be seen, wandering carefully among the fields, refreshing and helping all like. Presently you will see the train coming along the line, as if sent to convey some great soul to see this sight."

Leaving the Vale we will turn to the 13th century Parish Church which my father describes as "one of beauty and strength ", which in his boyhood was lit by gas and contained seats like "calf-pens, shut in by a door to every seat and so high that only adults could see across the church ".

The inside plastering was rough and badly in need of repair and the organ small, the finely carved oaken roof, however, must in contrast, have been all the more conspicuous in its beauty.

My father related that when a child his mother left him alone at home whilst she attended Church. Guessing where she had gone he wandered into the Church and down the aisle looking helplessly at the closed doors for his mother's pew. However, a young woman took pity on the lad, and, lifting him over the partition, placed him in the seat beside his mother.

There is a point, which is worthy of note, concerning the Old Town Cross previously mentioned. Some hundred odd years ago a charter was granted to the town of Sturminster Newton that if any inhabitant had a grievance which was genuine he was at liberty to stand upon the Town Cross and declare it, 'none having the power to stop him '.

It is of interest to note that either from timidity or ignorance of the fact, no one has ever been known to make use of this privilege.

As I intimated at the beginning of this article, much of the life and character has receded from this town. As in the industrial, so in the religious and political world, fervour has died down.

Counter attractions no doubt explain the laxity in attending Church and Chapel and perhaps the equality and freedom of the present day has wiped out the bitterness and old excitement of the political fight, but from 1866 to 1924 Sturminster Newton was " the hub, holding the political wheel of North Dorset ".

The result of the Poll was declared from the doorstep of the Old Boys' School and thousands gathered from the surrounding villages to hear the result of the elections.

There was swearing, jeering, coarse political jargon bawled in raucous voices, drunken brawls and fights not confined to men alone, but women, incensed, would roll up their sleeves and fight out some argument over the price of bread or beer.

The result of the poll is no longer declared in Sturminster Newton and the only survival of the old excitement at election times is a little heckling at political meetings.

Those old characters which are so much a part of the place are fast dying out and there are none of like calibre to take their place.

Individuals as such become fewer and more far between as the years go by and, no doubt, in years to come the stamp which marked the countryman and the dweller of the market town, will have worn itself away and there will be little left to distinguish the farmer from the city clerk.

DORSET SUPERSTITIONS

IT HAS BEEN SAID THAT NO PART OF ENGLAND is more prone to belief in the supernatural than certain parts of Dorset.

This is undoubtedly true for the ' old wives' tales ' still linger in minor superstition till the present day.

I was informed by an old lady living at Sturminster Newton that her brother had seen a man leaning on some railings on the bridge with his head buried in his hands. On being asked what was the matter he replied in desolate tones, " I zid a cross-eyed 'ooman vust thing this marnin'. Now I shall have bad luck all day."

The cross-eyed woman evidently savoured of the witch idea which was prevalent in Dorset less than fifty years ago.

I was told that a man at Stalbridge had complained that he had been ' overlooked ' as all his pigs had died.

At Gillingham, about the same date, a man applied for Parish Relief, stating that he was unfit for work owing to the fact that he was ' overlooked ' by his sister-in-law.

Still in the grip of this phobia people were afraid to pass the house of a certain woman at Tarrant Rushton whom they considered a witch. They would go two miles out of their way in the dark to avoid her.

It seems scarcely credible that just before the last World War a doctor in practice in the Blandford district reported that all the illness in the village of Winterbourne Houghton was attributed by the inhabitants to a woman living there who was a seventh child of a seventh child and therefore a witch.

The common antidote to witchcraft of drawing the blood of the witch, is of course well known. Hardy makes reference to this belief in " The Return of the Native " where Eustacia Vye is pricked by a needle by Susan Nonsuch in order to counteract the spell she is supposed to have cast over Clym Yeobright.

The villagers at Houghton used to waylay the witch in the dark, spring at her with a knife and then fly for their lives.

The doctor, previously mentioned, was often called out at night to attend to the severe cuts received by the witch.

It was strange indeed that the feeling of common humanity was thus superseded by fear and superstition.

Charms were sometimes employed such as horse-shoes over the door and here I plead guilty to having had one over my own back door, placed there by my father's hands, and on many a country cottage wall there may still be seen this token of good luck to those who live within.

China dogs, too, so often seen upon the mantle-shelf of the Dorset cottage, were supposed to counteract the evil spells of any 'overlooked'.

Witches, like Father Christmas, were reputed to have been able to come down the wide old-fashioned chimneys and here a pig's head stuffed with pins was often placed to drive the witch away.

An old Dorset woman herself told me that in the chimney at the house where she had lived as a girl there was found a bullock's heart stuffed with pins, and it is reported that "in 1884 a bullock's heart filled with nails, pins and thorns, was found in a chimney near Bridport." *

A certain amount of superstition hung around the birth of infants. It was considered lucky to plunge new-born babies into a cold spring. There was one at Cerne Abbas which was reported to possess wondrous powers of bringing good fortune.

The plunging of the infant into the water was considered more effective if performed at dawn.

This was probably a survival, in a different form, of the ancient custom of votive offerings to Pagan gods.

It was thought to be unlucky to carry a new-born infant from an upstairs room to a downstairs room. It should first be taken to another room upstairs.

Babies should not be weighed before they had lived three months or their finger-nails cut before they were twelve months old.

* Bournemouth Daily Echo May 16th, 1941.

If a boy was born at, or just before, the new moon, it was considered an ill omen.

There were various queer notions of bringing luck to a young baby ; one to spit in its eyes, another to dip its feet in the first fall of snow, which would prevent chillblains.

Then, should it cry at baptism this meant good luck and if fretful, an emulsion made from hare's brains would prevent its crying.

Apparently, a hundred years ago, even the clergy were not immune from superstitious beliefs for the following story was given to me as authentic.

In 1893 a young man was returning to his home on a very dark and foggy night, after having visited the girl of his choice, when he had the feeling that something or someone was following him.

Turning, he saw a wraith in the shape of a large ring like a child's hoop which dogged his footsteps for nearly a mile.

As he neared the Church the wraith suddenly disappeared into a gap in the Church wall.

The young man, both alarmed and mystified by his experience, recounted the story to the Vicar.

The latter replied, " Well, my man, if you had said, ' In the Name of the Lord, why troublest thou me ', and followed through the wall you would have been guided to some secret which may now never be disclosed ".

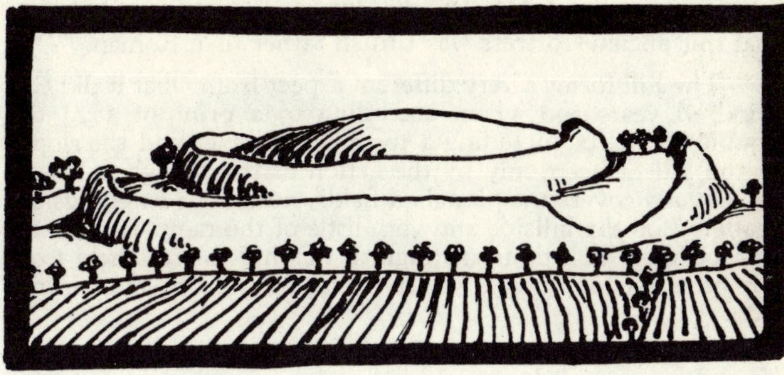

WOODBURY HILL AND ITS FAIR

THE ANNUAL FAIR held at the top of Woodbury Hill (half-a-mile North-West of Bere Regis) was at one time the largest in England. It lasted then from the 18th till the 23rd of September, and combined both business and pleasure.

This site was particularly well chosen for a large fair owing to the extensive flat top of the hill (from ten to twelve acres) and the magnificent view of the countryside which it commands. To the south may be seen Flowers Barrow, Burden Hill, and Gallows Hill, to the east the whole range of the Purbecks ; to the north-east Badbury Rings and in the far distance, the white cliffs of Scratchell's Bay and Freshwater on the Isle of Wight, are, on a clear day, distinctly visible.

On the north-west Bulbarrow and Grants Head may be seen and due west Weatherbury Castle, near Milbourne, stands clearly in evidence.

There has been some dispute as to whether this ancient structure was a British or Roman Camp as it is not actually on the Roman road of the west (The Icen Way), and as no Roman remains, although discovered nearby on Kingston Down, have been unearthed on Woodbury Hill, the conclusion drawn is that this ancient fortress was British rather than Roman.

The hill forms a very different aspect from what it did two hundred years ago when, according to a print of 1724 the double ramparts, including a fosse, were intact and the slopes of the hill defaced only by the action of the plough. Now a thick wood covers the ploughed fields, numerous dwellings are scattered on the hillside and very little of the rampart remains. In fact, there is little to distinguish this hill-fortress now from any other wooded height which overlooks the Dorset country-side.

Hutchins supplies a tradition as to the origin of the Fair, given him he says by an old lady whose family had lived for many years at Bloxworth.

The story goes that a pedlar travelling in the West Country with a pack of cloth in his bag was caught in a heavy storm and got thoroughly soaked. By the time, however, he had arrived at the top of Woodbury Hill, the storm had ceased and the sun shone. So, taking out the cloth, which was also saturated with wet, he spread it out to dry in the sun.

The advent of the Pedlar and his cloth quickly reached the villagers and they came just to inspect and then to buy the cloth which they soon saw to be of particularly fine material.

The pedlar, pleased with the sale of his cloth, came again the following year to the same spot, armed with material for purchase. Having a second time met with success he came year after year, joined by other traders for the sale of their goods on the top of Woodbury Hill.

As the business grew, a Charter was granted in the reign of Henry III, 1216 and so the Fair began.

It opened with Wholesale Day when traders, many of whom had come from Birmingham, Norwich and London sold various commodities such as cloth, cheese and hops. Next came Gentle-folk's Day which was the high light of the whole proceedings. The County nobility came from far and near in their carriages, gigs, four-in-hands, landaus and equipages of all descriptions to take part in the entertainments on the hill.

The village children would line the roadside to watch the arrival of these illustrious personages, proud to receive a smile from some fair occupant of an open landau, or glad to pick up the pence scattered lavishly from the hand of a Country Squire.

The beginning of the pork season was here celebrated by a feast of this viand appetizingly roasted for the occasion. Oysters, too, now in season, were consumed in large quantities and, even till this day, oyster shells are unearthed from time to time on the hill.

One of the entertainments on Gentlefolk's Day was an amusing kind of advertisement for leathern breeches when the lads of the neighbourhood were shaken into their new breeches by an ancestor of a maker of these garments in Puddletown.

On the third day, known as All Folks' Day, the fun of the Fair reached its height and many of those present gave themselves up to a reckless gaiety which ended in drunkenness and debauchery, the Parish Constables unable to cope with the lawlessness which ensued.

After this came the sobering effect of Sheep-fair Day and lastly Pack-and-Penny Day when all goods remaining were sold very cheaply so that nothing was left to be carried away.

On each day of the Fair horses were sold and altogether the amount levied from the business of the Fair amounted to £100 annually, in those days a princely sum, which found its way into the pockets of the Lord of the Manor.

Like most of the country Fairs that of Woodbury Hill has dwindled. Gradually the five days were reduced to two and the business became negligible. Up till three years ago the Pleasure Fair survived but now, this too, is no longer held. There is a tradition that there was on the hill, centuries ago, a deep well known as the Anchoret's Well, reputed to harbour a golden tablet which gave to its water strange healing powers. To drink of this water people came, it is said, from miles around on the 21st September. The pilgrimage was probably made by Roman Catholics in honour of the Nativity of the Virgin Mary and the money offerings made at the drinking of the water were handed over to the Abbot of the Tarrant Monastery.

There are also said to be, on the western side of the hill, the remains of the foundations of a Church which was dedicated to Saint Anchoretta, this being the mother Church of the one in Bere Regis to-day, St. John the Baptist.

Although there is still a deep well on the hill, it is no longer used and is considered not to be the ancient well of the Pilgrimages.

In fact the glory of Woodbury Hill has almost faded. It is remembered to-day merely as a prehistoric camp or the scene of bygone merriment immortalized by Thomas Hardy in " Far from the Madding Crowd " and " Tess of the D'Urbervilles", where old John Durbeyfield refers to " Greenhill Fair ".

AMONG THE DORSET GYPSIES

I HAVE ALWAYS BEEN INTERESTED IN GYPSY LIFE so, when the Romanies camped near my Dorset home I went amongst them all I could and learnt of their ways. I found them very friendly and quite willing to talk.

Their ideas were primitive but their wits were sharp and and they generally managed to get the best of the bargain in their dealings with the 'Gorgios' (non-Romanies).

They took great delight in being photographed especially if the subject were a mother suckling her infant. "'Tis lucky, me lady," they would say, "to be took at the breast."

I remember, when I handed a Romany mother the picture of herself feeding her baby, how she held it away from her and gazing rapturously at it, said, "I wouldn't part with it for £50!"

Indeed, it was a grand photograph. The mother's head was thrown back, her eyes alight with obvious pride at the infant clinging to her naked breast.

After that I had many applications from the gypsies to be taken especially in this way.

Another much cherished photograph among the tribe was one I had taken of a gypsy's first little girl sitting in her pony trap on the top of a bundle of rags.

Once, one of their children came to me and said, " Will you come and take our baby, me lady, he's going to die ? "

I was beginning to know their ways by then so I said, " Tell me when the baby's dead and I'll come." Needless to say the child never returned.

Another occasion I remember was when the gypsies were told to move off from an encampment they had made on the property of a well-to-do farmer.

The latter had sent a message to that effect by his bailiff, or someone in his employ. On being told to move they said, " You tell he the Big Book say only poor folk go to heaven. So there's no chance for he ! "

I have known them pack up their belongings and move off after being ordered to do so, till they considered sufficient time had elapsed for the police to get well away, then they would come back again and set up their tents in exactly the same spot.

I took it into my head one morning to wander out at daybreak and surprise the gypsies before the camp was astir but I had forgotten that their dogs would betray my presence. There was a quick sharp bark and instantly heads popped out from every direction, from tents, from caravans and from between the shrubs where some of the Romanies had slept, fully dressed. When they saw it was I they bade me a respectful ' good morning ' and withdrew.

I can remember once coming upon them unexpectedly at the top of Bulbarrow Hill in the midst of a grand feast of roast pork and potatoes. They made me right welcome and placed a cushion on top of a bucket for me to sit on.

There was certainly an absence of cutlery and china but

there were clean table cloths spread on the ground and the gypsies ate with relish from tins and cans of all descriptions.

I noticed near where I sat two children happily delving for snails in salmon tins, using for this purpose thorns they had gathered from the hedgerows.

Once I happened to come upon them just after a heavy storm. Clothes were spread everywhere on bushes and hedges, for the rest it might have been a nudist colony. Children were running about, their brown bodies completely naked. Spoiling the illusion, however, an older girl, I noticed, had draped her body with a curtain.

I had been walking one day with a friend through the dead bracken over the common and when we saw two adders my companion killed them both immediately. Shortly after this we met some of my gypsy friends. We informed them of what we had done and asked them if they would care to have the dead adders as we knew they used their fat for effecting cures.

For some reason they refused the offer but asked when we had killed them. On being told that it was but a few moments ago one of the Romanies, looking round towards the sun, said, "You have killed your enemies."

On another occasion I met a gipsy with her child and, noticing that the latter had an open wound on its hand, I asked the mother if she was going to do anything about it, "Well, me lady," she said, "'twill be riper tomorrow, then I shall put a dock-leaf on t' draw it out." Then she explained to me that one side of the leaf would "draw" out the wound and the other side would heal it.

The Vicar of a neighbouring village told me one day that as a means of getting the gipsy babies into the Christian community he had offered a shilling to the mother of every child baptized in his Church. After that mothers came frequently bearing a brown-skinned infant wrapped in a shawl. Each baby was duly christened and each mother happily received her shilling.

It wasn't till this had gone on for quite a while that the deluded Vicar discovered that he had christened the same infant a dozen times !

I was very amused, one chilly spring morning, as I took a walk around a gipsy camp to see the method one of the Romany mothers had adopted for washing her infant. She was taking a mouthful of water, holding it till it was warm and then blowing it over the baby's face. This she did over and over again, the child in her arms obvioulsy enjoying the process.

I had always wanted to know what actually took place at a gipsy wedding so one afternoon just before the gipsies moved off I went to their caravan about tea-time. Making me welcome as they always did, I was given a cup of tea by one of the Romanies who owned, besides his caravan or 'vardo', a pair of roguish dark eyes.

I had singled him out long before as being the most intelligent of the tribe.

" Will you tell me," I said, "about a real Romany wedding ? "

" Yes, lady," he replied at once, " but the custom is dying out in this country now."

" Never mind," I answered, "tell me about it just the same." So then he told me that most of the Romanies like a church wedding, though few of them can sign their name or know how to spell it.

After the service they have what they call the ' habber ' or ' big eating ', which consists of large quantities of roast pork (the pig they had bartered from a neighbouring farmer) which had been roasting gently for three hours.

Then the men drink beer, the women coltsfoot wine and the merriment begins. There will be vulgar jokes and 'sallies' and if the bridegroom can be made drunk enough for 'pamering' so much the better. " Pamering the bridegroom " means undoing the latter's clothing and pouring the contents of a jug of beer over his bare body.

After that the musicians of the party bring out their

fiddles and begin to play some old Romany songs which they all sing in raucous voices, more and more out of tune as time goes on. These revels will finish early, however, for tomorrow there will be the ' Rommerin ', the real Gipsy wedding.

My informant gave me a vivid description of this ceremony so that I was much impressed by its primitive beauty.

The next morning, he told me, after breakfast, the Romanies would form a circle, the children in front, youths and girls behind and the elders at the back.

The bride and bridegroom would stand in the middle of the ring, their hands palm upward towards each other. Then one of the tribe would make a small incision on the wrist of the left hand of the groom and the right hand of the bride and while the hands were bleeding from the wounds they were pressed together thus mingling their blood.

Now a skein of red silk which had been knotted by seven young virgins of the tribe was bound lightly around the wrists and hands of the united pair. Then came the betrothal kiss which means " You are for ever mine and for evermore I am yours."

A case of infidelity among the Romanies is almost unheard of. Their betrothal kiss seems to bind them eternally together.

Next comes the bridal song chanted by the whole company and the silken cord is cut. The couple then, hand in hand, run lightly together and leap over a pile of wood which in some cases has been set alight. This they call " jumping the Kash," and if taken clean, is supposed to indicate the strength and fertility of the young couple, giving fair promise of healthy young Romanies to come.

After this the couple return to the circle to receive a loaf of bread from the eldest member of the company, which is to be taken as a sign of plenty in their future life together. Then wedding gifts are presented to the groom, mostly silver and copper ornaments for the 'vardo'.

Then the couple run three times up and down two lines

formed by the assembly, at the same time being pelted by yellow ochre and flour which is supposed to bring them luck.

Now to wind up the proceedings they take out their fiddles once more, but before they start scraping out their rather tuneless songs, the Welsh harpist must play his sweet plaintive strains which is perhaps the only sound approaching real music which is heard throughout the ceremony.

The Romanies say there can be no luck at a wedding without the harp, because it is ' the chief instrument of heaven '.

They play and sing till dinner time, then a little more music and dancing and it is time to give the bride and bridegroom their send-off.

They receive a pat of the head from each member of the tribe and are told to pitch their caravan on a new site at least ten miles away, so they will start another clan of Romanies with *all* this rich tradition in their blood.

I thanked the obliging ' Romany Rye ' for all he had told me and wished him God-Speed. Next day the whole company trekked,

I missed them, they were kindly folk. I know that if they ever come this way again they will remember me as I shall remember them and we shall still be friends.

THE GIPSY'S FUNERAL

MARY ANN BARNEY WAS DEAD.

For years she had sold clothes pegs, flowers and brushes in the neighbourhood of this West Country town where she was a familiar figure with her little pony-cart hawking her wares.

Last night all Mary Ann's wordly possessions had been piled into her little trap, then according to tradition it had been set on fire like the Viking ship of some ancient warrior who had died in the glory of battle.*

And her little grey pony was shot.

Now none of her belongings were left except her body and the clothes that wrapped it for decent burial. Her husband and all her tribe had insisted upon full funeral rights, the bell must toll, the burial service must be read and the body laid to rest in consecrated ground, for all of which the gipsies had

* A survival of the custom of ancient tribes of destroying all the belongings of their dead, in order to equip the departed spirit for the next world and to prevent the return of the ghost to haunt the premises.

paid to the last penny. Church and churchyard fees, the grave-digger and all concerned had been paid.

Now on the day of the funeral they were waiting in the Market Place for the gathering of their tribes from far and near to witness the burial of one of their own.

These early comers stood about or sat on available seats, some regaling themselves with a mug of ale outside the local inn.

They were a motley crowd, their ear-rings dangling, their babies slung to their backs, some of the women wearing headgears of black lace like Spanish Mantillas, the men and boys with black scarves around their necks. All of them carried wreaths and bunches of flowers in their hands.

Presently shabby cars began to arrive laden with flowers at the back. These were the more prosperous Romanies who had come from many miles away.

Gradually they assembled, gipsies of all ages from seven different counties, till at last they were all there, ready to bear the coffin to the churchyard according to their custom.

When at length the hearse bearing the coffin and the chief mourner inside, approached the Market Place, every man and boy bared his head and placed his cap beneath his arm ready to join in the procession, but these Romanies who had waited for so long were baulked of their intention.

The hearse did not stop.

They could not follow in procession behind their dead. The gipsies were angry and disorganised. They did not know that it was the husband who had given the order to drive straight to the Church.

Not being able to keep up with the hearse they had straggled as best they might to the churchyard and now surging to the Church door lifted up their voices in angry protest. Why, they demanded, why could they not have the decent funeral they had paid for. A kind of mass hysteria ensued. The knowledge of their numbers giving them courage they shouted, screamed and wailed to the extent that the officiating clergyman standing at the Church door had no option but to commence the service where he stood.

At last the cries died down and slowly they followed the vicar who led them into church.

Here they sat silently, completely filling the body of the church, whilst the burial service was read. One face stood out among all the others at this strange assembly. It was deeply lined but bore the impress of unwordly wisdom and philosophic calm. She may have been an aged Gipsy Queen who held a place of honour midst her faithful tribes. She listened, with thoughts we shall never know, to each solemn word breathed over the dead.

The service over, the company now surged to the open grave anxious to place their flowers on the coffin. The churchyard by now was thronged with sightseers and coupled with the pushing and jostling of the gipsies it had assumed the aspect of a fairfield.

Scarcely giving the Vicar time to finish the burial service they pushed their way to be the first to lay their flowers in the grave. Then, determined this time not to be denied their age-old custom they took command of the situation. They each dropped upon the coffin a sprinkling of the earth.

Then some smote their breasts and set up a wailing reminiscent of Biblical times. This horde of gipsies was mourning the loss of one of their tribe, echoing the lamentations of their ancient forebears in the East.

Then they left the open grave, and sat anywhere on the churchyard wall and the grass. Some appeared overcome by the stupour of too much drinking before the funeral and sank down on the mounds of the graves.

Some of the mothers openly suckled their infants, some wept, a few, excited by the gathering of their clans, laughed and called to each other in their strange 'caterwaul' which is neither English nor foreign tongue, but a language which is peculiar to their kind.

Their funeral was over.

The sorrowing husband went far away to the hop-fields of Sussex to help him forget the dark-eyed gipsy to whom he had plighted his troth.

Tomorrow those Romanies who live in the district will come with flowers to lay on the newly-made grave. Then they will add cheap toys and pathetic little ornaments bearing illegible inscriptions to the dead gipsy.

In their own way they will try to solace the departed spirit on its lone flight to a distant gipsy encampment beyond the stars.

THE REDDLEWOMAN

WOMEN OF TO-DAY HAVE INVADED most of the professions to the extent that there is scarcely one in which the male has the prerogative.

Not so, fifty years ago. A woman then was frowned upon for having any desire to leave the home to which she was a slave.

But the unusual vocation of the Reddlewoman was apparently pursued, at this time, by a woman, in the byways of our Dorset countryside.

She must even then have been a relic of the fast-dying custom of selling reddle to the farmers for the marking of sheep, as Hardy, writing of this period, speaks of the Reddleman as belonging to "a class rapidly becoming extinct in Wessex".

The unpopularity of the calling could no doubt be attributed to the disfiguring red dye which inevitably covered both the person and belongings of the one who followed this occupation.

Hardy described Diggory Venn, the Reddleman, in " The Return of the Native" as being "completely red ", and that "one dye of that tincture covered his clothes, the cap upon his head, his boots, his face and his hands ".

Surprising then was it to find a woman occupied thus in the sale of this lurid dye.

However, be that as it may, year after year this woman of my recollection came and pitched her tent on the same spot in the grassy lane. To the children of the neighbourhood she was wrapt in mystery. Was she a "gippo" ? Was she a fortune-teller, or witch ?

I can see her solitary little encampment now, her small dark-brown pony, tethered to the four-wheeled open van which matched in size, both the pony and the diminutive tent and was a bright red in colour.

A fire of sticks blazed outside her dwelling and often on our way from school we used to gaze fascinated at the enticing scene before us.

We both hoped and feared that "she" would emerge from the little dark opening of the tent. We knew the occupant was a woman as rumour had gone around the village that she had been seen driving her van. She wore, we were told, a black hat and skirt and a red shawl and that when she drove her van she was big, but now, looking at the little tent we believed she must, like Alice in Wonderland, have taken a magic potion which made her shrink to a size which befitted her home. Otherwise how could she be confined in such a small enclosure !

There was one in our group, however, who stoutly declared that the woman inside the tent was neither witch nor fortune-teller but a kindly soul whom her mother had told her sold reddle to the farmers for marking their sheep.

We did not want to believe her. We liked to think of this female nomad as a witch-like individual who brewed charms and magic potions in the little black pot we could see on the fire.

Mysterious clanging sounds issued from the tent. We stood transfixed, our wide eyes glued to the opening.

Would a claw-like hand obtrude itself to beckon us to our doom ? If so, mesmerized as we were by our own imagination, we should, I verily believe, have followed to our own destruction, like the children lured by the Piper of Hamelin.

The clanging sounds ceased. There were a few seconds of silence, then, quietly, the occupant of the tent emerged.

We stared speechlessly. She was incredibly large. She wore the black hat and skirt, and red shawl. Her face was wrinkled like the skin of a russet apple but her eyes twinkled with the friendly humour which children recognise at once. Her hands were a vivid red.

We were no longer afraid, but at the same time our disappointment was acute.

" Who—who are you ? " I ventured. For answer she showed us her hands and we saw again their brilliant dye.

Then she looked from one to the other at our little group and laughed. " I'm sorry to disappoint you," she said, " I'm the Reddlewoman."

ALL ROUND ARCHIT.*

'TIS A MISTAKE T' BE *too* PARTICULAR, I tell 'ee, especially when you be in the mind o' courtin', zoo if you be waitin' for the perfect maid, take my advice an' gie it up. That maid ain't never ben barn.

Now when I were young I were that cautious I zampled a good round dozen avore I made up me mind, I went right on the brink, you mid zay, wi' each o'em—till, "Steady, me zon," I zaid t'meself, "She 'oon't do," and regardless of her feelins I did turn 'er down.

F'instance, there were Maggie. She were nice enough t'look at, an' middlin' good tempered but 'twere her voice I couldn' abide, raspin' it were. No, I thought t'meself, I likes a soft voice t'sooth me down. Fancy havin' 'er a-squawkin' all day like the wind drew a comb. So I looks elsewhere.

Then I met Gertie, who you mid zay were plain and

* Orchard.

whomely, but ready and willin' nevertheless, but I soon vound out that 'twas Gertie did want t'do the courtin'.

Ah, I thought t'meself, she be too eager be half. Why, 'tis the hay runnin' after the hoss! *I* likes t'do the courtin' and *I* likes t'name the time an' the place. As my wold father used t'zay, 'A man'll turn away from a too ready bride.'

Well, I took a turn wi' Annie, small and bright-eyed she were an' stood just as high as me heart. Now I've a-vound 'er at last, I thinks t'meself. All went well for a time, till one evenin' when we was strollin' along the country lanes Annie were took wi' a fit o' sneezin! She whipped out o' her pocket a dirty handkerchief.

I never took Annie out again, nor told 'er the reason why, but I wanted me wife t'be spick and span an' me house as clean as a bright new pin.

Now when I met Clara we took t'goin' out reglar. She were pretty t'look at an' neat an' tidy. She were always bright an' cheerful, not too fat an' not too thin.

Our courtship progressed be leaps an' bounds, an' I began t'think serious o' tyin' the knot. Then Clara, bein' o' the zame mind as meself, says, "Come t'tea next Zunday."

Knowin' what I do now, I often wish I'd never a-gone t'house but married Clara quick avore I'd a-met 'er mother, for 'twere Clara's mother this time that frightened I off.

No, I thought t' meself, I couldin' abide *thee* for a mother-in-law.

Why, she did vuss an' vidget like a broody hen till she did very nearly make I zick. "Be you in the draught, me dear? Don't 'ee zit t'near the door," she'd zay. "Now, do'ee 'ave a bit more, you ain't made hafe a tea!"

"Clara idden very strong," she said then, turnin' to I. "She niver been used t'hard work neither. I always did zay that my daughter ought t'marry a man who could afford t'make 'er a lady."

I knowed then that if Clara and I were wed, 'er mother 'ud be for iver on our doorstep, lookin' and pryin' in our affairs.

Zoo when I zaid ' Goodnight ' I told Clara as how I shouldin' be comin' again.

Mind you, I didn' like partin' wi' 'er for she were nice in 'erself an' worth two o' 'er mother, but many's the time since as I zaid afore, I've a-wished I'd a-married Clara avore I went t'house.

After that I vlit like a bee from vlower t'vlower, I zettled for a bit then off t'goo, for each o' 'em were bezet wi' zome liddle failin'.

Oone did talk t'much, another were too close-mouthed. Oone did sniff an' another did zuck 'er teeth, an' oone, a nice liddle maid in other respects, used t' cham when she did eat 'er vood.

At last come the day when I zaid t'meself, ' Garge, me bwoy, if thee doesn't hurry up thee bisn' gwine t'have nobody at all.''

Zoo now I gits it into me head that the best thing for I t'do was t'turn a blind eye and a deaf ear to all their liddle failin's an' *I* made up me mind I'd have the next one that did take me fancy.

Zoo when Polly come trippin' down the lane all amiles, an' dimples, wi'out more ado I axed 'er out. Then I hurried up an' popped the question quick, an' avore either she or I knowed where we was, we was up at the alter rails.

Not many weeks went by avore I vound out that all Polly's nice liddle ways avore we were wed wadden the real Polly at all.

She were sharp-tongued, quick-tempered, mean, graspin' an' selfish. She wanted 'er own way from mornin' t'night an' if I didn' gie in to 'er I couldn' bide in the zame house.

I'd a-ben took in proper wi' 'er beguilin' ways, 'er dimples an' smiles.

How I wished I'd a-married Clara, Annie, Maggie, or any oone o' the dozens I'd a-vound fault wi'.

What 'ud I care now for a fussy mother-in-law, a dirty pocket handkerchief, a raspin' voice !

A sniff 'ed a-ben music in me ears compared wi' Polly's cuttin' tongue.

Ah, why must a feller always learn the hard way! What I put up wi', nobody but meself d'know. I spent all me time a-dodgin' Polly's temper. I done things that I'd niver done in me life avore t'keep on the leeward zide o' the tyrant I'd a-brought t'me house.

All she did mind were keepin' the place wi'out a speck o' dust. She couldn' abide children but the house were her god.

" Garge," she'd say, " Take yer veet off the curb," and " Garge, you've a-stepped on the surrounds. Goo an' get the duster an' polish'n up again." Like the girt vool I were, I'd do what she zaid, for I were afraid t'rouse 'er spite.

One day she called out just as I were a-comin' home, " You can't come in, I be cleanin' up," and I 'ad t'bide on doorstep till she'd a-vinished her job.

'Ouse-proud she were an' no mistake.

Ay, but Providence is kind—she was took. All on a zudden she were took, an' I were a free man oonce more.

I'm lonely betimes, but I can do as I d'like. I can put me veet on the mantlepiece, an' dray on me pipe. I c'n read me paper in peace. I can eat me vill an' roast me toes, but the best o'me resent blessin's is, if I be minded, I can zit and do nothin' at all.

Zoo 'ere I be t'gie warnin' t'they who do look for a wife. If you vind a maid wi' zome vault outstandin', don't be too particular, but overlook 'n, you'll get used to'n in time, but if s'be you d'vine oone that d'show noo faults at all, then be sure she's wuss than all the rest. Avoid she like the plague.

Ah, learn a lesson from I, me sons, for do'ee zee, I went all round archit a-huntin' but I picked a crab at the last.

VARMER BRICKELL AND THE GHOST

Related by Wold Garge in ' The Travellers' Rest '

VARMER BRICKELL had just a-ben t' Christmas Market an' there's noo doubt about it he'd had a drop t'much for he'd a-met volk he had'n a-zid for years and he'd a-handed 'em all a toast o' whiskey an' beer till narn a-one among 'em were sober.

By the time he started whome-along 'twere past the midnight hour, for Varmer Brickell had a'bed in the pub till closin' time.

When at last he were astride his wold grey mare, he could zee two or dree o' everything about'n. 'Twere a bright moonlight night an' the shapes on the road an' the shapes in the vields did gi'en a turn an' he 'ad a vunny veelin' down the back o' his spine.

Varmer Brickell zaid that all the time he bed thinkin' about the divil-ghost that volk did zay did haunt the cemetery and look betimes over the cemetery gate.

Now Varmer Brickell knowed quite well that thease story weren't true, leastways, he knowed it when a-wer sober, for volks had a-told 'n 'twere a hoss, standin' stock still looking over the geate, wi' the moon a-shinin' behind 'n. A hoss, mind you, an' never a divil-ghost at all.

But poor old Varmer Brickell, now that his brain were vuddled wi' drink, could only think o' the divil-ghost till he did shake in 'is seat on the back of the wold grey mare.

Then the varmer looked behind 'n an' there a-zid a girt, ghost a-chasin' his hoss an' he only a vew yards behind 'n !

" Oh ! I be chased be a ghost ! " he yelled out, " 'Elp me, zomebody, 'elp me ! "

Then a-lashed up his hoss and galloped 'n all up Black-close Hill, an' turned into the wood to the path t'lead 'n whome.

Now Varmer Brickell, well nigh zober, plucked up courage to look again behind 'n. " Thank God," he zaid, " he's gone," an' sure enough he were.

Zoo now he let his mare goo down to a jog-trot and Varmer Brickell hummed a tune he were that glad t'be free o' the devil-ghost at last.

He turned his hoss t'the left then trotted along droo the wood an' then t'the right again which brought 'n out into the road once more.

Now the minute the varmer got ont'the road his fears come back an' leanin' down on the hoss's neck he took a look behind 'n an' there again he zid the ghost a-volleyin' his hoss an' he.

He broke out into a cold sweat, he nearly fainted. He made a vow in 'is heart that if s'be he got whome safe, he'd gi' up the drink an' goo t'Chapel o' Zunday nights. He'd never sware noo more !

At last he got back whome. He jumped off his hoss an' out of the carner o' his eye he could zee the divil-ghost had a-jumped down wi'n.

Zober at last, Varmer Brickell snatched the ridin' whip vrom beside the stable-door an' slashed out right an' left at the ghost who'd a-tormented 'n for s'long. Forgettin' his promise never to sware again the Varmer let out all the words a-knowed an' zome he'd never used a-vore.

" Lawkes a-mercy ! " called his wife, pokin' out 'er head from the bedroom window, " whativer's t'do, Reuben ? "

" 'Tis the divil," says Reuben between the lashins o' the whip, " the divil-ghost that frightened me out o'my wits."

" Why, father, you stupid wold vool," zaid his wife, " You be a-beaten yer own shadow. Come on t'bed, do 'ee."

THE WRONG MAN

MOST DOSSET MEN 'ave a-got all their wits about 'em but young Tom were always a bit slow on the uptake, although zometimes he did come out wi' a bit o' wit be accident.

I'll tell 'ee a tale he did often tell an' slap his thigh and lafe that hearty that once I zaid to'n, " Don't 'ee know, Tom, 'tis on'y vools d'lafe at their own volly ? "

" Ah'," 'e said, " d'take a wise man t'make a vool ! "

Well, Tom were a tiler be trade an' his work took'n about all over country.

Oone day, he were sent t'Southampton t'do a day's work and the pore feller had a job t'vind lodgin' for the night. He tramped the streets till 'is veet did ache but narn a place could he vind.

At last he come upon a lodgin', but, he were told, he'd have t'sleep wi' a black man.

" Oh, dear," Tom zaid, " I don't like the thought o'it."

There! 'T'ill be all the same in the dark," a-zaid, whether he's black or white."

So Tom took the lodgings, thinkin' 'twere better than trampin, the streets.

Avore he went t'bed he asked the landlord to call'n early so's he'd be up in time t'git to his work.

Now the lan'lord an' the black man thought they'd play a trick on'n, so when a-were zound asleep they blacked 'is face an' hands, then let'n bide till 'twas long past 'is time t'be up.

Then the lan'lord come thumpin' on the door. "Git up, Tom, quick!" he zaid, "I be that sorry I forgot to call 'ee avore. 'Tis eight o'clock."

Tom jumped out o'bed, an' wi'out stoppin' t'wash, an' wi'out a mouthfull t'eat, he rushed out o'house an' down street as vast as 'is lags could carry'n.

On his way he passed a girt mirror in a tailor's shop and cotched a glimpse o' hisself.

He stood stock still and stared. Then a-called out in a shaky voice, "Oh, my blessed. They've a-woke the wrong man!"

A 'DOSSET' MAN IN LONDON

Another of Garge's Tales

TOWN VOLK D' OFTEN THINK that we country volk be t'thick t'zee drew a brick wall, but we baint, I zay, we baint.

Hark t' this tale o' how I tricked a Londoner.

I'd a-gone up t' London for a liddle outin' for I'd always made up my mind that I'd zee London town avore I died.

The vust place I'm a-goin' t'look at is St. Paul's, I says t' meself, so I axed the vust man I zid goin' the zame way as I, how t'get there.

He looked at I, condescendin', and zaid, " I'll show 'ee, I'm going that way meself."

Now, I thinks to meself, I'm goin' t'have a bit o' fun wi' he !

He d'think I be soft. I'll soon show'n I baint.

Then I steps it out t'keep up wi'n.

" You be in a hurry, baint 'ee," I zaid, " be you catchin' a train ? "

" Oh, no," he zaid, "it would'n do for a Londoner t'move at your pace." But he slowed down a bit all the zame.

" I zay," I axed 'n all on a zudden, " Be you a Cockney born an' bred ? "

" Oh, yes," he answered, " for many generations back."

" Well, then, I'll gie' 'ee this half-sovereign," I zaid, an' I handed to'n a bright new shinin' coin that he slipped into his pocket avore you could zay ' Jack Robinson '.

Then we stepped along together wi'out a word an' I thought t'meself, if thease grimy black buildin's be London gie I the yellow buddercup vields O' Dosset. Then, all at once me companion zaid, " Look, there's the dome of St. Paul's ! " And sure enough, there a-were, like a gurt bee-hive agin the smoky sky.

Then I stopped, took off me hat and scratched me head. The volks did frown at I vor blockin' up the gangway. " Jist up from the country," I 'eard a man zay, pointin' back at I wi' his thumb over 'is shoulder.

" What's the matter ? " me friend asked.

" I baint sure," I zays, " that you be a Cockney born and bred."

" I be ! " he zaid, upon my word an' honour. I was born within the zound o' Bow Bells."

" Well, then, I'll gie'ee a sovereign for that half-sovereign, so hand'n back while I get out me purse."

He handed the half-sovereign back. I took 'en, put 'en in me pocket, then I looked the man full in the face.

" I know now," I zaid, " that you bain't nar Cockney. If you was a Cockney, you would a-zaid " Gie I thick sovereign," avore you'd a-parted wi' t'other coin."

" Good day," I zays, an' on I goes t'zee St. Paul's Cathedral.

GROUND UP A-VRESH

MY UNCLE CHARL WERE A HOSS DEALER an' many's the time I've heard 'n tell the tale o' how he sold Wold Tramp the carthorse to Varmer Biles.

'Twere like this yer, Uncle Charl bought a cart horse which were wold in the tooth but not yet gone a-past work. His teeth were long an' his head were grey. Anybody could zee wi' only hafe-an-eye that he'd zid a good twenty zummers or more.

Now, Uncle Charl always zaid that in hoss dealin' an' love, all is vair. If you could trick a man into buyin' a hoss, he zaid, the blame should be on he who were vool enough t' buy 'n.

So they zet t'work an' viled down 'is teeth till they showed but eight year. Then they mixed up zome dye t' match the colour o' the hoss's coat in his younger days an' painted his grey hairs.

Wold Tramp looked all ground up a-vresh and 'ud pass for eight years old.

Now between you an' I and the geate post, Uncle Charl told I once that he'd a-learnt these liddle tricks vrom one or two women he'd a-knowed in his time.

" What can be done wi' women," says Uncle Charl, "can be done wi' hosses."

So he sold the hoss t' Varmer Biles an' he vetched a goodly price. There were no doubt about it, Varmer Biles were a-took right in an' thought as how he'd a-bought a hoss wo'd zid but eight zummers in the buddercup vields.

Just about a year later Uncle Charl had some business t'do again wi' Varmer Biles.

" Charl," the varmer zaid, " I can't make it out, thick hoss I had from 'ee last year 'ave turned as grey as a badger."

" Oh," says my uncle, scratchin' 'is head. " You don't zay zoo."

" Ees," zays Varmer, " 'Tis true, an' 't'ave put twenty-year on to'n."

" Well, now," me uncle zaid, " I think I can give 'ee the reason for that there. I bought thick hoss from a varm where he'd a-ben bred and trained. He'd never left the Varm avore, do' 'ee zee, an' 'tis my belief he's a-grievin' for his vust an' only whome."

WASHINGTON'S OWN HONOUR

WI' ALL DUE RESPEC' TO HIS MEMORY, I d'often wish I'd niver heard the name of Garge Washington.

The trouble began when I were a bwoy at school an' I were vound out when I'd a-told a lie.

I 'ad a sharp cut wi' the cane an' told t'bide in. "I'll talk to 'ee after school," the maister zaid.

I shall niver forgit 'is words, "Masterman," a-zaid, "wheniver you be tempted t'swerve from the truth remember Garge Washington. *He niver told a lie.* Follow his example. Understan'?" The he gied me another cut wi' the cane t'drive it 'ome.

"Speak the truth an' shame the devil," a-zaid, "an' remember,

'Liars portion is t'dwell
In the deepest pit o' hell'."

Well, iver since then Garge Washington 'ave a-tormented

the life out o' I. T'this day if I d'goo a hairs-breadth from the truth there's Washington at me elbow. " Come on," he d'zay, " own up. That idden quite right what you just ben a-zaid ; all the truth, please. Spet it out ! "

Then, wi' me face s'rid as a beetroot, I zays the words over again an' puts the matter right.

The trouble is Washington d'git at I in all manner o'ways. " Tedd'n only in words," he d-zay, "you can tell a lie wi' deeds. You got off the bus t'other night wi'out payin' the conductor. I know he were upstairs at the time, but you should have gied yer fare t'some o' the chaps zittin' b'the door. He could have a handed it in. You must pay double next time."

Zoo, next time, I gits on the bus I hands the double fare t'the conductor, " That's for t'other day," I zays, "when I got off wi'out payin '."

" Thanks very much," he zais, and slips it in 'is pocket.

" Niver mind, you'm cleared," whispers Washington in me yer.

Oone day I were doin' a bit o' shoppin' for the wife an' I vound when I got out o' shop that they'd a-gied me too much change be a ha'penny.

" Goo back," orders Washington, "an' hand it in. That idden' your property."

Back I goes, " You gid me too much change," I zays, " be a ha'penny," and I hands it back.

The girl cocked 'er eye-brow, slid the coin in the till, an' gie me a look s'much as t'zay, " Be you quite right in the hid ? "

Oh, yes, I be often led into situations where I d'look proper voolish but 'tis the banner o'truth an' I must keep'n vlyin' at all costs.

I shall niver fergot what a vool he made o' I when I took a liddle outin' down be the sea t'other day. I thought to meself I'll 'ave a deck-chair a' bask in the zun.

Now the ticket collector must just have a-ben round for

he never come near zoo after about hafe an hour, I got up an' sloped off. That were a stroke o' luck, I says t'meself. Then all at once Washington poked I in the ribs. " You niver paid for yer chair," he zaid, " Tha's the zame as tellin' a lie."

" No, tidn'," I zaid.

" Yes, 'tis," he zaid. " Goo back, vind the ticket collector an' pay up."

I knowed he wouldn' gie me no peace zoo back I went t' the front an' looked round till I vound'n.

" Here's the money for me chair," I zaid. " You missed I out," an' I handed'n a hafe-crown and waited for me change.

" Thank you," the collector zaid, "who told'ee 'twere me birthday ? " He slipped the hafe-crown in 'is pocket and went off quick's lightnin'.

T'other day I were wakin' along an' spotted a handbag lyin' in the road. I couldn' believe me eyes—I stooped down an' picked'n up. He were made o' real leather.

Me han's did tremble at sich a rate that I couldin' hardly undo'n, me vingers were all thumbs.

When at last I got'n open I vound a lace-edged pocket handkercher, a tiddy liddle bottle o' scent that did smell like real vi'lets an' when me clumsy vingers got open the middle I vound a wad o' bank notes, I counted 'em out, there were thirty o' 'em. Thirty quid in notes. Why 'tis a fortune, I zaid t' meself. I'm come in for a fortune !

As it happened I were down on me luck at the time an' I thought on me mother's words, " The Lard'll provide." Tha's what she always used t-zay. " The Lard'll provide, me zon."

'Tis an answer t'prayer, I zaid t'meself, an' I danced round on the spot wi' glee, then I carefully put the bag under me coat an' turned back t'goo whome wi' me treasure.

Ah, bit I had'n a-bargained wi' Washington. I hadn' a-gone many steps avore he were a-proddin' I in the ribs.

" Goo back," a-zaid, "goo straight to the Police Station an' hand over thick bag."

" No, I bain't," I zaid, " Vindin's keepin's."

" You take he straight t'the Police Station," a-zaid, " If you d'keep'n you be a-tellin' a lie."

Zoo off I went an' handed'n in.

" Leave'n here," the sergeant zaid, "an' I'll let 'ee know when he's claimed. 'Tis nice to know we got oone honest man in the plaice."

" Zometimes," I zaid, " I'd wish I were the biggest liar in creation."

The Sargeant cocked 'is eye-brow. " 'Tis Washington," I zaid, " he d'plague the life out o' I."

A vew days later there were a thunderin' knock at me door, an' there stood the policeman.

" I'm come t'gie 'ee a reward for yer honesty," he zaid an' 'eld out a pound note. " The bag was claimed, an' the lady sent 'er thanks."

" Virtue's own reward, that it, Sarg ? " I zaid, thinkin' o' t'other twenty-nine, Then I 'eard a voice, faint but unmistakeable, " Well done, Masterman, keep'n vlyin'."

Well, a vew weeks went by an' I began t'think that Washington 'ad a-vinished wi' me. He d'know I be an honest man, I thought t' meself, now he's gwine t'let I bide.

But I made a mistake about that there for oone night he played the worse trick on I that he'd iver played avore.

I woke up wi' a start in the middle o'the night wi' me wife asleep be me zide.

" Wha's up ? " I muttered. Then I let out a groan for I knowed what 'twere.

" Masterman," I 'eard a voice zay, "you've a-broke yer marriage vows, an' you d'know it. 'Tis the wuss lie a man can tell. Wake up yer wife an' confess yer zin at once or you be a lost soul."

I broke out into a cold sweat. " I cain't," I whispered, " I cain't."

" Do what you be told," zaid Washington, " 'tis yer only chance."

" Emmie," I zaid at last, knowin' I were beat, " Wake up, I got zummit t'tell 'ee."

She didn' take no notice, zoo I gied 'er a dig in the ribs. " Emmie," I called out, " Wake up."

" What d'ye want t'wake I up far ? " she zaid, " I were just in me fust sleep."

" Emmie," I whispered, " I got a confession t'make to'ee."

" I always thought you was keepin' zummat back," she said. " Out wi' it."

" Well," I zaid, " 'Twere oone night in the black-out, I . . . . I . . . . kissed a girl. I kissed 'er 'ard."

" You what ? " Emmie asked. Then all at once as though it struck 'er funny, she laughed out loud.

" Well," she zaid, "all I can zay t'that is, it served 'er jolly well be rights ! Goo on t'sleep."

She turned over an' in two minutes she were zound asleep again an' I were veelin' s'big a vool as a man could veel.

" Dang it," I zaid, " I'll gie he notice t'quit."

But 'twere no use. He'd niver let I alone for long.

One day I met Pason. Pason an' I did often 'ave a chat together. We was good pals, so t'speak.

Now, I thought, t'meself, I'll zettle this matter once an' for all, zoo, " Pason," I zays, " Where do you think Washington is ? "

" 'Twas in America when I was a boy," he said.

" Ah, I don't mean that," I zaid, " I d'mean, Garge Washington."

" Oh ! " Pason zaid, " I see ! You mean where is the soul of George Washington ? "

" Tha's right," I zaid. " Ud you zay he'd a-gone to Heaven ? "

" Why, certainly," Pason replied. " If ever a man was fit for heaven he was."

" Well, then," I zaid, " I'll tell as many lies as I be minded and goo to t'other place," an' I marched off leavein' poor wold Pason wi' 'is eyes a-poppin' out o' 'is head.

But I 'ad'n gone many yards avore I were pulled up sharp an' I heard a voice zay 's clear as a bell, " Masterman, 'tis noo good for 'ee t'talk like that there. I've a-made a honest man o'ee, zoo I got 'ee now, in this world an' the next."

THE MOSSY BRIDGE A-THIRT THE STREAM

Not many volk 'ave trod
The liddle bridge I know,
For green upon his path
The springy moss d'grow.

When children come t'play
Down in the vlowery glade,
They jump the runnin' brook
Or bare their veet an' wade.

An' young men in their prime
Do take oone easy stride
An' vault the pebbly stream
To t'other grassy side.

But for the likes o' me
There bain't noo other way
T'span the shallow stream
Where children love t'play.

'Cept where my liddle bridge
Do zeem t' beckon me
T' tread his mossy stone,
An' keep'n company.

A DORSET GRANNY

I had the pleasure of meeting an old Dorset woman whose kind is fast dying out. I am not allowed to give her name so I will call her Granny, as the villagers do.

Granny is pure Dorset, not only in her speech but in personality as well. The folklore of the county is part of her make-up and her vivid imagination colours her whole attitude to life.

When I first saw her she was wearing a fur cap and a cloak and walked with a stick. She was slightly bent but agile still, for all her eighty-five years.

She gave me a welcome and invited me into her house which should have been thatched, with a tiny rose-covered porch. Instead, her home was built of Purbeck stone and stood solidly facing the sea as blue that day as the Mediterranean. However I noticed, on entering, that Granny's personality pervaded the place and the atmosphere inside was that of the traditional Dorset Cottage, complete with oak settle, old-fashioned fireplace and family portraits adorning the walls.

There was her son, a slim straight lad, clad in khaki who was killed in the First World War and there, Granny said, pointing to the settle, was where he sat on the night before he went away, never to return.

Gradually the old lady's wonderful personality unfolded itself. Her beliefs were clearly defined and optimistic despite her tragic life-story. She believed in God and in a heaven where she would meet her loved ones. She also believed in Spiritualism as part of her religion and her faith in the occult was almost primitive.

Granny told me that she had left school at the age of twelve and gone to 'service'. Then she confided to me that her good looks had brought her trouble. Indeed, it was not difficult to imagine that in her youth she must have been strikingly pretty, for her features were good, her eyes a bright blue and her skin, even now, fair and smooth.

"Yes," Granny said, "the master of the house where she first went to work, although a married man with wife and family, pursued her to such an extent that she ran away."

In her next place, however, she was wooed and won by an adventurer who left her to face her trouble alone. Unable to keep her situation for long, the girl reached the verge of starvation and intended suicide. She was reclaimed at the last moment and eventually bore the child which died.

It was not till after the death of the child that the father returned and offered marriage, but the girl refused and married the man with whom she spent sixty years of wedded life. Quite recently they celebrated their diamond wedding.

Granny's husband was a builder and has apparently been successful but the old lady retains the indelible stamp of the Dorset rustic which she will carry to her grave.

During my short stay she related, in her broad and rich dialect, stories of crime and horror coloured with a superstition in which she obviously believed. She spoke of clairvoyants, and spiritualists and fortune-tellers with such conviction that for the time being I came under her spell. The old woman believed in 'second sight' and claimed that she herself was clairvoyant. Aware of her penetrating blue eyes this was not difficult to accept.

She told me how at one time she visited a spiritualist who said, "I see a blind man walking and with him a soldier". The blind man was one called 'Blind Garge' whom she had taken in as a lodger and tended till he died. The soldier was her son who had died in the first war.

The story of Blind Garge was pathetic. He was apparently a somewhat disreputable character when, out of the goodness of her heart, Granny in her younger days had looked after him for five shillings a week. He had been, in her own words, "bad for women" and a drunkard but now he was reaching the close of his life. One night he declared there was a knock on his wooden bed which meant that his end was near. He lay, an unlovely sight, disfigured by small-pox, his features coarsened by vice and brutality, but the Dorset woman with second sight bent and kissed him.

"Was that a Judas's kiss?" asked poor 'Blind Garge'. "No," replied the woman, " 'Tis the kiss of a child." That night he died and when the woman came to lay him out for burial, the evil and repulsive features of the blind reprobate had gone and in their place were the smooth contours of an innocent child. "Why," cried the woman, "This bain't 'Blind Garge', this be a beautiful boy."

There is one other of Granny's stories I should like to tell which she related with great relish and a kind of triumph. It centres around Oak Cottage, which still stands in the Purbeck village where the old lady lives.

A young squire, a gentleman farmer, had married a village girl but they did not live happily. The husband, in frequent fits of ill-temper, was wont to throw a glass of cold water in his wife's face.

One day, however, the ill-used young wife in desperation paid a visit to Jenny Ghoul, the wise woman who lived in Studland. The girl entered her dwelling saying she had taken shelter from the rain. "But," said the far-seeing woman, "You bain't come in out o' noo rain. You be come d'hear about thick young squire. I'll put a whip in thee hand t'bring'n t'heel."

Then the witch told her that next time her husband threw water into her face she was to ask him if he knew Oak Cottage in Windmill Lane.

Not many days elapsed before the girl was subjected to the same treatment from her husband as before. She obediently asked the question as instructed but it was not until a day or two later when she had repeated the words several times, that a change came over the cruel young squire and, as if impelled by some unknown influence, he offered to drive his wife to town, along the road beneath North Hill. Then, "What do you know about Oak Cottage?" he asked.

Finding that the mention of the Cottage had proved effectual in bringing her husband to his senses the girl once more visited the witch to enquire what her husband had done.

"Come again in a month's time," she was told, for Jenny Ghoul never wasted her words.

Exactly a month from that day the squire fell from a load of hay and broke his neck. His wife went straight to the witch and was told that her husband had murdered his aunt and buried her body at Oak Cottage in Windmill Lane.

Granny assured me that for long afterwards the cottage was haunted by the poor old lady's ghost. The rustle of her silk dress could be heard at nightfall. No one would live there but, said Granny, "To-day the ghost is never zid nor heard. He mid a-ben redeemed".

Yes, superstition and folk-lore are part of the aged woman's make up. She belongs to the past. The future grandmothers of Dorset villages will have no such heritage to hand to successive generations. Tradition is fading with the dialect and when these old folks have gone they will have taken with them something of Dorset which can never come again.

THE VETERAN ARTIST OF STUDLAND

It was with something approaching reverence that I interviewed Studland's veteran artist, Mr. A. H. Berens, who in his eighty-ninth year, still works at his craft.

I was shown into his long narrow work-room, where a heaped-up coal fire burnt red in the grate, although the spring day was quite warm. All around me were evidences of the artist's pursuits, panels of gold-painted lacquer work, wood-carving, pictures, brushes and pots. Hanging on a wall in front of me I saw a row of guns, long and heavy weapons which must have taken a deal of handling. On another wall, hung rather incongruously, I thought then, a photograph of Baden-Powell which must have been taken many years ago.

Presently, Mr. Berens came into the room. He was tall and distinguished and remarkably upright for his eighty-eight years. His complexion was delicate, his hands unusually long. There was something about him which bespoke the soldier as well as the artist.

When later I went into his studio and saw his display of gold lacquer work, Spanish and Oriental leather work, carving, water-colours and etchings, I knew that here, tucked away in this little village on the Dorset coast, was an artist of very high degree.

I marvelled both at his superb handiwork and his extreme modesty. The delicate beauty of some of the gold tooling, the beautiful design and colouring of the lacquer work, to my mind looked worthy to adorn the Temple of Solomon.

This versatile artist had besides wood-carvings, engraven brass and embossed leather, cases exquisitely painted in gold. I had learnt by now the reason for the big fire on a warm day. It was to keep the work-room at the required temperature of 110°, necessary to prevent this precious metal from becoming dull.

I was then shown into a small studio adjoining this one and there on the walls hung delicate water-colours depicting scenes from the beauty of Studland, the varied outline of the coast, the changeful colour of the sea, and the wild fowl that haunt the shores. There were also coloured etchings of great delicacy and an interesting study of the "Old Harry" rock in the days when "His Wife" stood proudly by his side.

It was of course, in the early years of this century that the latter disappeared during a storm which wrecked the Old Chain Pier at Brighton, but Mr. Berens has lived long enough in Studland to have seen the pair stand united and to transpose them to his canvas.

After this I saw albums full of photographs of scenes from the artist's past career, many of which depicted groups of boy scouts with their famous leader and founder. It was then that Mr. Berens told me that he had been scoutmaster to 122 boy scouts under Baden-Powell at Brownsea Island, where the movement first began. He had taught the boys, he said, to do everything but knit, and some of the designs in the work-room were specimens of their handiwork.

As the leaves of the album flicked over I noted a photograph of a blotter in powder blue, gold-tooled and painted, which the artist had made for H.R.H. Princess Mary.

Among the most interesting of the photographs were several of Mr. Berens in his younger days driving around in his four-wheeler drawn by four donkeys.

When I had seen his display of art, to my delight Mr. Berens began to talk about himself and Studland. He told me that he first came to the village at the age of nine. When he grew up he began to study art and was warned by his father that if he did not get a picture hung in the Academy before he was twenty-one he would spend no more money on him. The young Berens, accordingly entered, at the age of twenty, a picture 14 ft. by 12 ft. called "The Moonlighters". This depicted a study of lions and jackals. He then made off to Africa to avoid the storm, should he not be successful. The picture, however, was hung, so Berens was allowed to continue his artistic training and was in the schools for fifty years. He travelled the world over and declares he saw it at its best.

He had a picture hung every year in the Salon whilst he was in Paris (Julian's Academy), and another in the Schulters at Berlin during the four years he spent in Germany. He spent some time at the Antwerp Academy, returned again to Paris, and from there went to Japan and China. Whilst in China he lived in the jungle at the back of Singapore, which is now of course, civilized. For eight years he lived among the Arabs at Morocco south of the Atlas Mountains, and during that time painted the natural beauty of the desert. He showed me some of these pictures and I delighted in their warmth of colour. Then he referred to the weapons on the wall and told me they were guns from each Arab tribe. During our conversation I learnt that the artist had illustrated several of Hardy's novels and although he had not met Hardy himself, knew Mrs. Hardy quite well.

Mr. Berens told me quite openly that his return to Studland after his marriage was occasioned by the desire to get away from his mother-in-law. He chose Studland as being the most cut-off spot he could think of, for in those days there was no ferry and only a rowing boat for conveyance to the village.

Studland at this time was in its wild and natural state. The heath by the coast was a paradise for botanists and wild geese, duck and widgeon flocked around the coast. Falcons stayed to build their nests and rear their young on Pinacle Rock, and were seen at times plucking their quarry on the Agglestone Rock.

Mr. Berens can tell tales of the smuggling which was at its height when he returned to Studland. "Parson's Barn", a natural cave near "Old Harry", was ideal for hiding contraband goods.

Small farms dotted the cart-track to Redhorn and the fields were given up almost entirely to the growing of wheat which was

Tolpuddle.- The Martyr's Tree

ground at the water-mills at Ullwell and Arfleet. However, with the installation of bigger mills in Poole this village industry was crippled and the water-mills disused.

It is, according to Mr. Berens, the motor-car which has despoiled the beauty of Studland. "These motorists come," he declares, "throwing about their litter and carelessly causing fires to blacken the heath. I do not like the modern mind," he says. "To-day the young think only of themselves."

However, I noticed as I was talking at the gate to Mr. Berens that old and young passed a friendly greeting to my unusual companion. He raised his stick in salutation and I knew that, despite his somewhat cynical remarks, he loved his fellow men and the village where he had spent so many years.

The attractive house in which the artist lives was designed by himself and characteristically named "Full Stop". "I must come to a Full Stop," he says and so, after his wanderings all over the world he has chosen this beautiful corner of Dorset as his "Journeys' End".

THE MARTYRS OF TOLPUDDLE

It was in the February of the year 1834 that tragedy came to the little village of Tolpuddle, seven miles from Dorchester, when the six farm labourers now known as the Tolpuddle Martyrs, were arrested for having "participated in the administration of an illegal oath". After their arrest they were taken to Dorchester Gaol, from there to the convict hulks and then to the penal settlement of Australasia for a period of seven years' transportation.

In actuality these six men had met together beneath the trees on the village green in the early hours of the morning and after their toil in the evening, to discuss a means of obtaining a living wage to support their wives and families. They had already approached the local magistrate, counting upon the support of the resident clergyman, but without success. By way of protest against their stand for higher wages the farmer had reduced their pay from 9/- to 8/- per week and now after their appeal to the magistrates had further reduced it to 7/-, threatening yet another reduction to 6/-.

The leader of the labourers, George Loveless, a self-educated man of high intelligence and integrity and also a Methodist Local Preacher started, in October 1833, a "Friendly Society of Agricultural Labourers" in Tolpuddle. Their meetings were held regularly, usually in the upper room of Thomas Standfield's cottage. It was here that the ill-fated meeting was held which led to their arrest.

Thomas Standfield lived here with his son John, and these two men with George Loveless, his brother James, James Hammett and James Brine, were the six men who were sentenced to seven years' transportation to the penal settlement for administering to the members of their union an illegal oath.

It seems that the government had determined before their trial that these men should receive the sentence of transportation, for they used unfair means to twist the statute of the law to condemn the labourers for seditious intentions and illegal procedure of which they were not guilty.

From the time of their arrest to the passing of the sentence the labourers bore themselves with dignity and fortitude.

George Loveless, owing to illness, was not able to travel with the other five to the prison hulks at Portsmouth where they remained for several weeks. The hulks were old wooden warships used as floating prisons. In one of these called the 'York' the five were confined. The newcomers were given the lower deck where they were forced to remain when not at work and slept at night, they were never free from their chains at ankle and waist, their clothes, bodies and beds were infested with vermin and every kind of disease swept the foul habitation. Punishments were given for the most trifling offences, rations were reduced, the weight of the irons increased and the prisoners flogged with unspeakable cruelty. It is given as authentic that one prisoner, though not of these five, who had escaped from one of these hulks, was brought back, ordered to receive ten dozen lashes in view of all the other convicts, then, naked he was bound to the gratings and lashed for an hour with a knotted raw-hide lash. After collapsing on deck he was taken to the hospital ship where he was 'brought round' by the application of a salt dressing to his mutilated back.

On April 11th, 1834, the five labourers sailed from Plymouth on board the convict ship *Surrey*, bound for New South Wales. George Loveless, now sufficiently recovered to be removed from Dorchester Gaol, was not allowed to join his comrades, but, after a period in the 'York' hulk, he was shipped aboard the *William Metcalfe* to Van Dieman's Land, Tasmania, 700 miles from his friends.

These convict ships were even worse than the hulks and known as 'floating hells'. The discipline was such that many attempted to commit suicide and those who died on the way were considered lucky. Forms of punishment used were the branding iron, the iron strait jacket, the spiked collar, a short chain to keep the convict stooping, a cat-o-nine-tails tipped with pellets of lead, and the brine-bath into which the convicts were plunged after their flogging.

In the case of a ship-wreck the prisoners were locked below when the vessel was filling with water. Should any attempt to mount the ladder to the upper decks they were fired upon or had their throats cut.

The result of this inhuman treatment was to turn these tortured men into beasts of prey. James Hammett and his companions chained to these wretched victims, herded together in a foul atmosphere of dirt and disease, were driven to the verge of despair. They, however, managed to retain their sanity and arrived on August 17th at Sydney Harbour, to complete their sentence.

George Loveless, after similar experiences in the *William Metcalfe* reached Tasmania on September 4th of the same year, where owing to his exemplary conduct, his treatment was apparently merciful and no outstanding brutality is recorded. The other five fared much worse in New South Wales and were treated as slaves, entirely at the mercy of their masters. They worked in chain gangs, and were given insufficient food and clothing. In some instances they slept on bare flagstones without covering of any description. For no apparent reason they were, on occasion, locked up in prison without food, then handcuffed to a chain and marched through the streets like wild beats.

Always hanging over their heads was the possibility that on

some minor offence they might be sent to darker hells or still worse penal settlements. James Brine was, in fact, ordered to Norfolk Island, the most dreaded of all these places but the ship was prevented by a gale.

James Hammett, whose experiences are the least known, was sold to a master 400 miles distant for the price of £1. This journey he made on foot, alone through the bush, with rations sufficient only for twenty-two days.

Meanwhile in this country agitation for the support of the distressed families and for the release of the condemned men never ceased. There were meetings of the unions and petitions presented to the government. Finally a procession of Trade Unionists headed by Robert Owen passed through the streets of London to Whitehall to lay before Lord Melbourne, the Home Secretary, the petition for release. This, however, he refused to accept. It was not until the agitation had lasted for nearly two years that it pleased His Majesty William IV to grant a full pardon to the six Tolpuddle Martyrs.

Eighteen months later, September 11th, 1837, and exactly four years from the date of their trial the *John Barry* bearing the Dorset heroes, with the exception of James Hammett who returned later, reached the shores of England. They were given a public welcome at Plymouth and a warm reception at the Antelope Inn at Dorchester. Later on Easter Monday a procession in London was organized concluding with a dinner at 'White Conduit House' given in their honour.

The five comrades were then installed on pleasantly situated farms in Essex. In 1839 they were joined by James Hammett. Here they lived happily for several years in a close friendship strengthened by their mutual suffering.

In the year 1844 they decided that Canada had more of future prospects to offer them and in consequence, again with the exception of Hammett who returned to Tolpuddle, the five friends emigrated to Canada. Here with their wives and families they lived, true to their democratic principles and the cause of Methodism. They were all buried in Canadian soil. A humble headstone marks the grave of George Loveless and serves to commemorate his simple faith and dauntless courage.

Six cottages, well designed and fitted up, stand as a memorial to the Martyrs and at the same time house in comfort six aged village folk.

Beneath the trees where so many of the meetings were held a shelter and a seat bear an inscription to the memory of the six Dorset Men. On the outer wall of Thomas Standfield's cottage, where the fateful meeting was held, a tablet is erected to their honour.

James Hammett's grave, the only one of the six to be buried in Dorset soil, is marked with a stone which bears the inscription :

> "James Hammett, Tolpuddle Martyr, Pioneer of Trade Unionism, Champion of Freedom."

More than a hundred years have passed since the last of these Martyrs was laid to rest but ensuing generations have reaped the benefit of that sacrifice and the farmworker of to-day is well paid, well-housed, well fed, and well content.

ORME ANGUS

the Inspired Schoolmaster

It is regrettable that the author of "Sarah Tuldon" should have been almost forgotten, but such is the case. The reason may be partly that a contemporary of Hardy must, of necessity, be eclipsed, and also that, having made his mark as a Dorset writer, the creator of "Sarah Tuldon" through force of adverse circumstances, then turned his attention elsewhere.

Orme Angus (John Charles Higginbottom) came to Wareham as a pupil-teacher in 1885 and lived at Northport House near the railway station. He was a native of Marples, in Cheshire but Dorset became his adopted county and, inspired by the rustic charm of his surroundings, he felt impelled to embark upon a literary career.

His first book was "Jan Oxber", a collection of short stories previously written for magazines. Others followed, "Love in our Village", "Zike Mouldom", etc., but it is the vivid and life-like story of "Sarah Tuldon" which is generally acknowledged as his masterpiece. The book is alive with humour and pathos and the story of the pretty and dominating Sarah is told with real insight and charm.

It is difficult to realise and impossible to detect that the author is not of Dorset origin. The dialect and rustic character are faithfully portrayed and the atmosphere of the book is impregnated with the spirit of the locality. Though the author does not 'locate' his scenes as Hardy does, there is every reason to suppose that the 'Barleigh' of "Sarah Tuldon" is Bere Regis.

Orme Angus was frail in body but strong in spirit and entered with zest into whatever he undertook, whether on the cricket pitch or in the study. He taught for twelve years as an assistant at the Wareham Board School, at the same time pursuing his absorbing hobby of writing.

He then attempted to support his wife and himself by his pen. It was on this account that he was later to become the victim of poverty and ill-health for he soon proved that belief in one's own powers is not sufficient to earn a livelihood.

"Sarah Tuldon" was given a full-page review in the *Spectator*, the editor (St. Lo Strachey) being a personal friend of Orme Angus, and a cheap edition of the book was issued but, even so, the amount received by the author totalled less than £50. No hint of sadness or despair, however, creeps into the work of Orme Angus.

"Sarah Tuldon" not being a financial success, the author then, in order to attract a wider public, wrote "The Prime Minister", a book of totally different setting and character, but, although Angus himself considered this book "extraordinarily good of its kind" the general opinion was that he knew far less of statesmen and their ways than of the Dorset peasant-folk. In consequence he was persuaded to write a sequel to "Sarah Tuldon" and after greatly over-taxing his fading strength Orme Angus produced a lengthy sequel of 134,000 words which he called "Sarah Tuldon's Lovers", this, although well received, and in the author's opinion a finer book than the original, proved no more successful financially.

Dire poverty then followed almost to the extent that the next meal was uncertain. The struggling author clung to the hope that his writing would finally bring success. He applied for advance of royalties on "Sarah Tuldon" but this was refused as only between 500 and 600 copies had been sold. He had written a score of short stories that year but only one had been accepted. "Am I becoming a worse writer," he says of himself, "or is my luck out? I cannot believe the former".

It was at this time, on the advice of his friend, St. Lo Strachey, he applied to the Royal Literary Fund for monetary aid. He was granted £50. This proved, as he had hoped, a tonic, and, despite ill-health he wrote for nine years more, but he produced nothing in any way comparable with the early life story of his Dorset heroine.

It will be as the author of "Sarah Tuldon" that Orme Angus will be remembered by his friends for never again did he recapture the freshness and winning charm of this engaging Dorset story. Here his simple style shows to best advantage, and his homely characters most real. The undaunted spirit and incurable optimisim of the author is revealed in every line. He believed in himself and, despite set-backs and ill health, retained his steadfast faith to the end of life.

He died at his home in Wareham in March 1919, at the age of 52. Apart from his friendship with St. Lo Strachey he was little known in the literary world. He was, however, given the honour of becoming a member of the Dorset Field Club, as a recognition of his attachment to the County.

He was buried in the Churchyard of the Parish Church at Wareham having lived for over 30 years in this little Dorset town.

Orme Angus was at times a powerful writer who took the Bible as his model of literary style. He would commit whole chapters of the book of Isaiah to memory, believing that from this source his inspiration would come. Undoubtedly his work was influenced by his study of the Scriptures.

He did not aspire to great heights, neither did he plunge into the depths but was content to write in simple style of homely characters. His love of humanity made him write with insight and sympathy of the rustic folk he knew so well.

He did not seek fame, but his faith in himself as a writer led him to believe that he would eventually be recognised. It was indeed a tragedy that, not only was he disappointed in this respect, but having written books which were well reviewed and praised by over 40 critics, they did not bring in sufficient for his maintenance.

Granny Cousins.

He deserves to live in memory if for no other reason than that of the dedication of his life to the pursuit of his art. Dorset people especially owe him a debt of gratitude and if he does not rank among the literary giants he showed a greatness of spirit which deserves renown.

GRANNY COUSINS

the last of the Knockers-up in Poole

There are still many "knockers-up" in the industrial north, but here in the south of England the custom, always rare, has now become extinct. For this reason I will tell you what I have been able to find out about Caroline Jane Cousins, the last of the "knockers-up" in Poole.

She was born in the village of Morden, near Poole, but was never registered, as in those days the registration of infants in the country was very lax. She was reared in a labourer's cottage in the most frugal style. In those days it was the ambition of every cottager to have a pig in a sty and a side of bacon suspended from the chimney. Cuts were taken as required, the remaining portion becoming smoke-dried as it hung over the log fire which never went out.

'Granny Cousins', as she came to be called, would often recall, in later life, the days when she lived in the country. She would tell of the making of a meal in the cheapest and most economical way.

"You put yer piece o' bacon in pot," she would say, "an' then when he've a-cooked a bit, put in yer cabbage, then whack up yer dough enough for the family and put he in on top. Tha's Skiver Cake, that is, an' good for 'ee, too. But don'ee drow away the water 'tis biled in. You drink that there an' 'twill keep away all manner o' diseases."

It was in the years before the first World War that Granny Cousins "knocked-up" the workers in the twine and pottery factories of Poole. She would go her rounds six days a week from the Quay to the Gas Works, embracing Lagland Street, Thames Street, Strand Street, Taylor's Buildings, Emerson Road and the High Street.

Work in the factories started at six, summer and winter, so that the old woman began her duties long before daylight in winter time. She invariably wore her 'curtain bonnet', white apron and shawl and carried in one hand a long pole for tapping on the windows and in the other a lantern to light her way. She also carried a whistle so that she could communicate with the police in the event of being molested.

For the sum of threepence weekly she made herself responsible for the early-rising of these workers, but made it a point never to call twice. She gave her sharp rap upon the window-pane, and if she received no reply, passed on to the next, expressing what she thought of these "slug-a-beds" in no uncertain terms.

During the day-time Granny Cousins did her share towards making the twine. She payed out the 'tow' or fibre to the spindle which stood in the "Ladies Walking Field" or "Rope Walk" as it was then called. The tow was tied round her waist in bulk and was attached to the spindle which was turned by hand. Then the old woman walked slowly backwards paying out the tow as she went. As the wheels of the spindle turned they divided the fibre into strands and twisted them together into twine, hence the name "Rope Walk".

With all these long hours on her feet it is not surprising that Granny developed a corn at the bottom of her foot. This she doctored in her own fashion by wrapping around the bottom of her foot a piece of banana skin and leaving it there for three days and nights until the banana skin was black and the corn softened. It was easy then to remove the offending growth.

Apart from this minor discomfort the old woman ailed nothing at all. She no doubt owed her good health to her extremely regular habits and enormous quantities of food. Her life was ordered entirely by the clock. (She possessed a battered and rusty old alarm clock which had no doubt accompanied her on her rounds of "knocking-up".) At exactly the same time every morning she arose and started on her rounds and at exactly the same time every night she sat down to her cup of cocoa and four large tea biscuits. Her intervening meals were taken with the same precision and to keep up her strength she would drink the water in which her vegetables were cooked.

After the first World War she did no more "knocking-up" and gave up her work at the twine factory. She must by then have been very old indeed, but no-one knew her age, not even herself.

She had always been one upon whom life's knocks had made little impression. Her only remaining son, Solomon, had had both legs cut off in an accident unloading sand and gravel during the construction of the new railway from Poole to Hamworthy Junction. This disaster his mother had taken quite philosophically. Her life, no doubt, had made her hard, and when Solomon died she had shown but little sign of grief.

Neither did she show much affection for her grandchildren (her daughter's three children). Maybe it was only her way, for she was a strange old woman who did not wear her heart upon her sleeve. She had a way of talking at great length to no-one in particular, her gaze straight before her. If anyone interrupted her discourse with a question, she would shut-up 'like a clam' as they say in Dorset, and say not another word.

She did, however, bestow great care and attention upon an enormous oak-geranium which was kept in the 'front-room' window of the house where she lived. This she watered and tended, and fondled its little blue flowers. The huge plant kept the light from the room, but Granny Cousins would not hear of its removal.

It was at this time that the old woman joined the Salvation Army to which cause she remained faithful until her death. Granny Cousins received no old-age pension, as she had not been registered and so was maintained on the "Parish". She had no home of her own but, characteristically, showed no signs of self-pity and lived contentedly in the humble lodgings she had acquired with her friend.

There came the day, however, when even Granny Cousins' strength began to wane and she was taken to the local infirmary where she eventually died. It was by a strange coincidence that the giant oak-geranium withered and died when the old woman's coffin was brought to the room where, in life, she had tended the plant.

By stranger coincidence still there was at the same time a birth and a death in this small dwelling, for upstairs a child was born while Granny Cousins lay awaiting burial in her unmeasured coffin below. She was buried by the Salvation Army who swelled the numbers of her mourners which would, otherwise, have been surprisingly few.

Nevertheless, this strange old woman will figure in the history of Poole for a photograph taken when on her rounds, complete with bonnet, apron, lantern and pole, is hung in the local museum. She deserves to survive, not only by reason of her unusual occupation, but on account of her stoical and uncomplaining acceptance of her unrewarding toil.

BILLY, THE PARROT OF HONEYMEAD LANE

Billy's plumage and size mark him out as a native of India, but he is now thoroughly English and Dorset is his adopted county. His colours range from dark green to light, bright yellow, red, blue, grey and torquoise. He is larger than an Australian or Brazilian parrot and more brightly coloured than an African. For forty-eight years he has lived with his present owner, Mr. Elkins, a veteran of the 1914-18 war.

When Billy first came to the Elkin's household it consisted of father, mother and son ; but now both parents have died and the parrot is the sole companion of the pensioner who lost his leg in the First World War.

When the weather is warm, Polly, as he is more often called. is to be found in his cage outside the back door. From here he entertains all and sundry with his witticisms, songs and hilarity. This, of course, depends upon his mood, for he is as capricious as a woman. He will sometimes lift up his voice in melodious song, soprano or tenor, according to his whim, or at times produce a medley from snatches of songs learnt long ago from the sailors on his long voyage from India. On occasion he will laugh uproariously, then drop into a soft humming like a woman at her work.

Perched here in this Dorset country lane he has identified himself with the creatures around him and echoes their cries. His mimicry is perfect. Billy will squeal like a pig, bark like a dog, baa like a lamb or call like the cuckoo in spring.

His vocabulary is extensive and it would seem that he had stored up in his sub-conscious all sorts of trite sayings which he cleverly reproduces at the right moment. For instance, a while ago, Billy was sitting in his cage at the back door, when suddenly and without warning a sparrow-hawk swooped down upon his cage with such force that it was killed in the act and fell dead beside the cage. The parrot was frightened to such an extent that he cowered trembling at the foot of his cage, ejaculating at intervals, 'Save, O Lord, Polly's going t'glory'. After his recovery from his fright Billy's prayer for deliverance was heard no more and he resumed again his puckish sallies at all and sundry as they passed down the lane.

Polly's accents definitely savour of the Dorset dialect and he often preludes his sayings with a long-drawn-out "Ah" like any Dorset rustic.

When in the mood for joking he will venture his favourite sally, 'Hoi ! What's madder? Nothin'?' When the coal man's cart rumbles down the lane he will whistle shrilly and when children on their way to school collect around his cage, he will sing with a reckless hilarity, beginning on a low note and ascending to a screaming falsetto.

Billy has always been single-minded in his devotion and only confers his favours upon one human being at a time. Whilst Mr. Elkin's father was alive it was he whom Billy allowed to stroke his head or shake his paw and it was upon him that Billy bestowed most of his affection. When the old man was taken away to hospital the parrot moped in his cage and said very little but when he came back he joyfully greeted him with "Hello, Polly's Arthur!" and sang lustily.

When at length the old man died it was touching indeed to see Billy's grief. He huddled for weeks in a corner of his cage, ate but little, sang and spoke never a word. But time healed even Billy's sorrow and gradually he revived and, like the wise bird he always was, transferred the affection he had given to the father to the son. Yet even now, at intervals he cries, "Father's gone out" in a plaintive voice showing the old man still lives in Billy's faithful heart.

In all his remarks the bird shows an unusual sagacity. He will call the cat or dog by name, "Come on, Floss," he will say to the dog and to the cat, "Hello, puss ! How's poor liddle tabbie?" When hanging outside the back door Polly sometimes feels chilly, then he will warn his master by calling out, "Frank, get Polly's hat ! Polly out back door".

When Mr. Elkins returns from a shopping expedition the parrot will greet him with, "What have 'ee got? That for Polly?"

Occasionally he will voice little platitudes—like, "You don't know what you're talkin' about," "That don't matter", or "That's enough o' that".

Billy has always shown an unerring instinct for danger. During the last war he sensed an enemy plane before those around him were aware of it, and crouched trembling in the corner of his cage. A few moments later the plane started machine-gunning at close range, proving his judgment to be correct.

Billy leads an orderly existence. He leisurely eats his meals, chewing each beak full with careful deliberation. After each meal he takes a little nap then, when in congenial company, starts his animated chatter or cheerful banter.

He is particularly fond of music and responds with his own tunes he has learnt from memory. He has a bright and beady eye with which he contemplates the world around him in serene detachment.

Towards evening his feathers, which, during the day have been fluffed out, settle down into a smooth and glorious sheen and catching the lamp-light, show to advantage the varying shades of his bright plumage.

Billy has lived fifty years. He is young yet, for parrots habitually live to twice that age. His future is unknown, at least to us, but, maybe, Billy who seems to know so much can see the long years that lie ahead and knows that at least some human will care for him as long as his heart beats beneath the gay colours of his wing.

N.B.—Since these lines were written Billy, alas, has died.

WAITIN' FOR JENNY

O, Jenny me dear,
I've waited s'long.
Do 'ee come quick.
Where be?

Each time I do hear
The snap of a twig,
I thinks t'meself
'Tis thee.

Yet 'tis but a bird
Vled out from his nest,
Or a cow zet voot
In ditch.

Or mid-be a mouse
Do stir in the hedge,
An' I thinks 'tis you,
You witch !

For a witch you be,
My sweet purty dear ;
You've a'cast a spell
On I.

An' all the day long
I think on your smile,
An' all the night long
I sigh.

O, Jenny, me dear,
I be nearly mazed.
Do 'ee come quick
T' me.

I've waited s'long
By the wold oak tree.
Jenny—O, Jenny !
Where be?

STINSFORD

Stinsford is a tiny village about a mile from Dorchester, consisting of Church, Stinsford House, the Vicarage and a number of farm-houses and cottages, but, of all Dorset villages, this one was chosen as the burial ground for the heart of Thomas Hardy.

No better spot could have been found, for this parish gave him birth and his boyhood and youth were spent in the vicinity. The best known and most delightful of his novels, *Under the Greenwood Tree* is centred around this sequestered village under the name of Melstock. The little old church of St. Michael is redolent with memories of the old string choir of which Hardy's father, grandfather and uncle were enthusiastic members.

One window in the south aisle of the Church is now dedicated to Thomas Hardy and on the west wall is a tablet to the memory of his three musical relatives.

Hardy makes mention of his father when a choirboy in the gallery of the Church. It was in the days when Lady Susan Strangways lived at Stinsford House. Her husband, William O'Brien the actor, had recently died. The attachment between them had been very deep and had survived since the time of their famous elopement in 1764.

"My father," says Hardy, "when a boy-chorister used to see her, an old and lonely widow, walking in the garden in a red cloak."

It was Hardy's grandfather who was tearfully requested by Lady Susan to build a vault "just large enough for us two". The request was carried out for the Hardys were devoted to Lady Strangways, she and her husband were buried together and a monument to them both was erected on the chancel wall of the Church. It consists of two oval marble tablets united by two hearts, after the style of a Valentine, suggesting their abiding affection.

Later, we get a description as an eye-witness of the burning of Stinsford House. Hardy was returning one September evening from Dorchester when he saw the home of the Strangways in flames. The furniture was on the lawn, servants perspiring and crying and figures in shirt-sleeves on the roof. Men were battering out windows to get out the things. "A bruising of tender memories for me," says Hardy, "I worked in carrying books and other articles to the Vicarage.

"When it grew dark the flames entered drawing and dining rooms lighting up the chambers of so much romance. The delicate tones of the wall-painting seemed pleased at the illumination at first till the inside of the rooms became one roaring oven and the ceiling fell, and then the roof, sending a fountain of sparks from the old oak into the sky."

In any mention of Stinsford Hardy conveys his deep feeling for his native place. *Under the Greenwood Tree* is impregnated with his love of this verdant countryside and his understanding of and sympathy with the rustics who dwelt there, for not only the novelist himself, but his father and grandfather lived in the cottage at Bockhampton in the parish of Stinsford.

Hardy's grandfather, who was a master mason, had settled in the cottage at Bockhampton in 1801. He was a great music lover and organized a band of musicians who played for the services in Stinsford Church, also at weddings, christenings and any such festivities in the village. His son Thomas, father of the author, assisted in all these functions, and when his father died, not only managed the business, but continued to direct the musical activities of the parish. He married Jemima Hand, a woman of dominant character and strong mind, who bore him four children, one of whom was the Dorset Novelist.

It was from his father that Hardy inherited his quiet, unassuming nature, his love of music and of the Dorset countryside. As a boy he often accompanied his parent when playing at weddings and parties in the village and for this reason it is easy to account for his intimate knowledge of their Christmas festivities described in *Under the Greenwood Tree*, and of the Carol Singers, who during their rounds on Christmas Eve led the Tranter's son, Dick Dewy, to his first glimpse of the village schoolmistress, pretty Fanny Day.

During his early manhood, whilst still living in the parish of Stinsford, Hardy describes his chief interest in life as being the three strands, architecture, study of the classics, and his love of the countryside. It was not until he had left Stinsford and settled in London that he wrote, in retrospect, this perfect village idyll. A more faithful portrayal of the Dorset rustic has never been penned. Each individual of the Melstock choir stands out in clear relief, his mannerisms, his dry humour, his steady determination to be given due recognition. His love of music, quaintly modified by touches of human vanity, marks each member as a personal study of the author. Even the half-wit, Thomas Leaf, who on account of his piping treble, was admitted to the choir, becomes a real and pathetic figure to complete the picture.

Towards the close of his life Hardy was a frequent visitor to his birthplace at Higher Bockhampton and to Stinsford. He was grieved to see that the cottage was becoming neglected. He also visited the churchyard. It was a spot extremely dear to him, for it contained the graves of his first wife, his parents and grandparents and some of the most intimate friends of his youth. On one of these visits to the Churchyard he cleaned off the lichen which had accumulated on the head-stone of George Reason, the shoemaker, so that the epitaph was more clearly visible.

Hardy loved every inch and every tree in this quiet place and, aware that it would be his burial ground, was known to have written in a letter to a friend, "I shall sleep quite calmly at Stinsford whatever happens".

He loved, too, the little church, and though admittedly agnostic, often attended the services, for his religious feeling was too deep to be dispelled by intellectual doubts, the church itself too closely associated with his own family history to be forsaken.

So it was that in the January of 1928, when Thomas Hardy died, his heart was buried in the grave of his first wife, beneath the yew trees in Stinsford churchyard, whilst his ashes were laid to rest in Poets' Corner in Westminster Abbey. A spadeful of Dorset soil, sent by a farm-labourer, was thrown over the casket showing that even his acknowledged greatness was inseparable from his allegiance to the poor.

BROWNSEA ISLAND

The early history of Brownsea Island is little known. It is recorded, however, that a Danish fleet conveying Danes from Wareham to Exeter in 1876 was wrecked off the coast of the island. It is known, also, that there are indications of Roman occupation as pottery and a Roman bath have been unearthed.

There is every evidence, too, that the possession of the island was taken over by the monks of Cerne Abbey soon after it was founded (supposedly by St. Augustine in the sixth century). The monks cultivated the island and maintained a chapel, priest and confessional for the spiritual needs of fishermen and ferrymen.

In the eleventh century King Canute, after his second invasion of England, sacked the monastery of Cerne and conveyed the plunder to Brownsea Island. He destroyed the chapel but afterwards made reparation to the monks.

It was not until the reign of Henry VIII, when Cerne Abbey was suppressed, that Brownsea Island becomes history. A blockhouse or fortress was built for the protection of Poole and the shipping trade. Poole was required to pay six men to "watch and ward" the blockhouse. Later the town was expected to pay the entire cost of maintaining and garrisoning the fortress.

In 1543 Henry VIII made a grant of Brownsea Island and its surrounding waters to John Vere, Earl of Oxford; the duty of watch and ward on the S.E. point was still maintained by Poole.

In 1576 Queen Elizabeth I granted Brownsea and Corfe Castle to her favourite, Sir Christopher Hatton, known as 'the dancing chancellor', having attracted the Queen at a masque ball. He was created Admiral of Purbeck and lived luxuriously at Corfe Castle.

The orchard and garden of Ely Palace were surrendered to Hatton by order of the Queen, the Bishop, however, reserved the right of free access to the Palace gardens and to gather twenty bushels of roses yearly.

Hatton presented the Queen with elaborate and costly jewels and opposed in Parliament the suggested marriage of Her Majesty with the Duke of Anjou. In 1584 he was accused by Mary, Queen of Scots, of being the Queen's lover ; the consequence of this was that Sir Christopher took action in Parliament advising her execution.

Hatton was made Knight of the Garter in 1587 and later Lord High Chancellor. Her Majesty's favour, however, was not maintained, for an estrangement arose between them on account of the Queen's demanding payment from a collection of tithe, which Hatton had considered his own. From this time Sir Christopher's health began to decline and in 1521 he died.

Brownsea Island in 1654 came under the influence of the Parliamentarians but the Puritan, Colonel Pride, soon withdrew his soldiers, who were occupying Brownsea Castle as he opposed any form of agreement between King and Parliament.

In the reign of Charles II the reaction from Puritan severity set in and Sir Robert Clayton, renowned for his magnificent manner of living, was made Lord of Brownsea by the "Merry Monarch". Sir Robert was a scrivener and citizen of London. In the year 1679-80 he was Lord Mayor of that city, and was considered one of London's wealthiest citizens. He was renowned for his lavish hospitality and it was said of him that his entertainment was such as 'might have become a king'.

It was at this time that renowned masters of 'musick' performed upon the lute, harpsichord, violin and viol d'amore (five wire strings played on with a bow) in the most exclusive London circles.

The dandified style of dress of the period is revealed in Pepy's entry in his diary : "The Lord's Day. Up : and put on my coloured silk suit, very fine and my new periwig bought a good while since but dursent wear because the plague was in Westminster when I bought it".

Sir Robert, apparently, did not live at Brownsea Castle but occupied a dwelling erected for himself nearby. The castle, owing to the State's preoccupation with sensual gaiety, became neglected and, like many other coastal defences fell into disuse. Great then was the alarm when in 1690 our Fleet was defeated at

Beachy Head by the French and the French Admiral de Tourville, with seventy-two ships of the line, was threatening Poole on his way from Brest to the Isle of Wight.

Thus with Brownsea Castle unarmed the burgesses of Poole were called upon for the defence of their town.

All those possessing arms were asked to bring them to the Town Hall for inspection and cleansing in readiness for immediate use. Four tremendous guns were mounted at the gates of the Town and a nightly watch of thirteen men instituted. Four men were appointed as 'a sea-watch or guard', two of which were in the King's Scouts and two at Brownsea Castle. The former were to give notice of any approaching danger and the latter to warn the town by the firing of a gun.

The French Admiral, to the intense relief of the Mayor and Corporation of Poole, made for lower down the coast and the masts of the French fleet were later sighted off the coast of Portland. Teignmouth, instead of Poole, became the target of the enemy.

It was fear of the plague which brought about the visit of Charles II to Brownsea Island of 1665, when the plague was rampant, he fled from London to Salisbury and from there on September 15th he came to Poole. Here it is recorded the Mayor, Alderman and Sheriff 'had the singular honour to attend on His Majesty at dinner', after his dinner the King, accompanied by his son, the Duke of Monmouth, Lord Ashley and several others were rowed in Colonel William Scutt's boat to Brownsea Island, where His Majesty took an exact view of the said island, castle, bay and this harbour, to his great contentment'. He returned in the same boat to the quay of Poole where he was handed ashore by the Mayor and went on foot to the house of Colonel Scutt.

King Charles did not land on the island, it is thought, on account of an antipathy which existed between him and Sir Robert Clayton. He did, however, borrow £30,000 from the latter "to pay the soldiers with", and omitted to return it.

On the death of Sir Robert, Brownsea Island passed into the hands of Mr. 'Auditor' Benson. This gentleman had a 'long and handsome pedigree' unfortunately tainted by hereditary lunacy. He was a member for Shaftesbury in the first Parliament of

George I. He took possession of the Castle as his dwelling, rebuilt it, adding a Great Hall which afterwards became the Music Room. He cultivated the island and added many and varied kinds of trees. Being an enthusiastic botanist he collected and preserved specimens of all the curious plants on the island and placed them on view in the Castle Hall.

Mr. Benson was a liberal patron of Art and Letters and a great admirer of Milton, a monument to whom he raised in Westminster Abbey. He gave an Oxford scholar £1,000 for rendering 'Paradise Lost' into Latin verse and in 1735 paid an author's debt of £200 and freed him from gaol.

In the summer of 1741 he entertained Frederick Lewis, Prince of Wales and eldest son of George II, at Brownsea Castle. Later in the same year he was overtaken by the hereditary mental disorder and, strange to relate, after his recovery, his intense love of literature had given place to hatred of the same degree. Two years later he died and was buried in his native town.

In the middle part of the 18th century the Island was owned by the family of Sturt whose ancestral connection with Dorset dates back to 1392. Mr. Humphrey Sturt practically rebuilt the castle, but preserved the Great Hall as it was in Mr. Benson's time, also the ancient staircases and carvings. He is reputed to have spent £50,000 on improvements of and additions to the castle and grounds. From 1754-1786 Mr. Sturt sat in Parliament for Dorset.

His second son Charles, who was an excellent yachtsman, succeeded him. He is described as possessing 'an excellent fortune, which with a liberal hand and benevolent heart' he used 'to benefit society and for public good'.

In the February of 1799 Charles Sturt, at the risk of his own life, saved the lives of a ship's crew, bound from London to the West Indies, in a small cutter called *The Bee*. The boat had gone ashore during a heavy gale on the sands near Poole and Mr. Sturt gallantly went to the rescue, his boat being several times filled with water, and he, and those with him thrown into the sea. He struggled against the breakers for some time nearly up to his neck in water but had the satisfaction of saving the lives of each of the crew and giving them the hospitable warmth and comfort of his castle home.

For this act of heroism Mr. Sturt was awarded in November 1800, the medal of the Royal Humane Society.

In 1817 Sir Charles Chad became the owner of Brownsea and made further improvements and additions to the Castle and grounds. He made a pheasantry covering several acres and built an attractive cottage on the north shore overlooking Poole, which was later used as a keeper's cottage.

In 1818, George, Prince of Wales, afterwards George IV, visited the Island as a guest of Sir Charles and was received by a salute from the Castle guns. The Prince was enchanted by the romantic beauty of Brownsea Island and remarked to his host, "I had no idea there was such a delightful spot in the Kingdom".

It was Colonel Waugh who bought the estate in 1852 and restored the castle adding a Tudor Gothic front of Portland stone. He erected the pier and watch-towers, the clock-tower and new farm buildings. He also built, at the cost of close on £10,000, the Church of St. Mary. This is a stone erection in early decorated style, consisting of chancel, nave and transept, with embattled western tower containing four bells. A particularly beautiful carved screen separates the nave from the tower, in which is the family pew and private entrance. The church can seat 100 people.

In 1901 Brownsea Island was sold to Mr. Charles Van Raalte and during his occupation in 1907 General Baden-Powell held his first camp of Boy Scouts on its shores.

In 1927 Mrs. Bonham-Christie, the present owner bought the island. A passionate lover of animals, birds and all wild life, Mrs. Christie wished her island to be a sanctuary for these creatures. Her plans, however, were temporarily defeated when some years ago a fire spread among the woods for several days, destroying trees, bushes and undergrowth and many of the wild animals she loved.

During the early years of the last war Brownsea Island was taken over by the Government and here refugees were gathered to be examined and fed before being passed on to other parts of the country. During the aerial attack on Poole, Brownsea fortunately suffered little damage.

To-day Mrs. Bonham-Christie is once more in residence on her island home and still retains her 'watch and ward' of the animal world.

WAREHAM

Wareham, situated about a mile above the junction of the rivers Frome and Piddle is one of the oldest boroughs in the Kingdom and, as such, is worthy of distinction. Bounded on north, east and west sides by ancient ramparts known as the "Walls" and on the south by the river Frome, the area thus enclosed is 100 acres. The main entrances were two gateways, one near St. Martin's Church, known as Northport and the other on the west, still called Westport. The walls are actually earthworks built up for defence in prehistoric times. It is thought possible that Wareham was captured by Vespasian during the Claudian invasion and the existing ramparts extended. They were undoubtedly originally much higher, for they were dismantled during the Civil War.

The Danes, landing at the mouth of the Frome, often raided the borough and although Wareham was said to have been the best fortified town in the Kingdom of Wessex, in 876 the invaders took full possession and held it for a year. At this time Wareham was considered a notable port, for the sea practically reached the town. With the retreat of the sea, however, its importance diminished and at the same time Poole rose into prominence.

There is every indication in the town of Roman occupation. The streets are laid out at right-angles resembling the Praetorian Camp at Rome. Roman pottery (Samian ware and Roman Quems) have been found, also coins of the early Emperors. A villa was unearthed at Furzebrook three miles away from the town and many of the roads are unmistakably Roman.

The walls command extensive views of the surrounding country. From the east, Wareham Harbour, Poole, and the Pine woods of the Arne promontory may be seen. From the south-east the Agglestone Rock, or Devil's Night Cap, is visible. Much legend has grown up around this rock. It was said to have been slung from the Isle of Wight at Salisbury Cathedral, by the Devil in a fit of anger. The Druids, too, are here reputed to have offered human sacrifices to their gods. In actuality this gigantic stone was left behind after excavations from the nearby quarry. It has much diminished in size by the action of wind, frost, hail and snow.

From the north Walls we see the Sandford Pottery which originally manufactured Staffordshire ware but now makes glazed pipes. Inside the north-west angle is the cock-pit which is known as the Amphitheatre.

The west gives a view of the Isle of Purbeck, the range of chalk hills which extend from West Lulworth to Studland, Corfe Castle, and Creech Barrow. From the highest point on the West Walls the Isle of Wight may be seen on a clear day.

A mile or so to the south-east of the town, a rare and beautiful specimen of flora grows over a large area, called ciliated heath. It is found nowhere else in the neighbourhood or in the country except Cornwall.

Creech Barrow is 637 feet above sea-level and dominates the heath. It commands a view of Portland to the west and Bournemouth and the Isle of Wight to the east. It has the appearance of a volcano, the shoulder on the south-east side resembling the mouth of a crater, but in actuality it is non-volcanic and consists mainly of clay, the summit being sandy. In contrast to the brown of the heath its green sward is marked and pleasing to the eye. There is said to have been on its summit a Royal Hunting Lodge in the reign of King John. The hill was an ideal view point for the location of the King's deer.

A part of the West Wall is named "Bloody Bank", as near by, five victims of the Monmouth Rebellion were publicly executed. Since then, however, came the "Great Fire" of 1762 destroying most of the town and at the same time wiping out most of the horror of its past history.

Wareham, in common with the rest of Wessex, is inseparable from the personality of Thomas Hardy. The town figures as Anglebury, so named by Hardy to reflect its antiquity. The two novels, *The Return of the Native* and *The Hand of Ethelberta* are both concerned with 'Anglebury' and its surroundings. The vivid description of Egdon Heath in the former novel has made it appear as one of the most vital characters of the book.

Mrs. Craik, the author of *John Halifax, Gentleman*, lived for a while at Westport, and writes of Wareham scenes and characters in *Agatha's Husband*.

Miss McFadden has also written of Wareham as it was in the 19th century, in *The Honest Lawyer*. By then the town had settled into a state of tranquility after the horrors of the Civil Wars and the Great Fire. "Market day," she says, "was an incident; fair day, an event. Beyond these excitements, the tide of life at Wareham moved slowly forward, like its own rivers, and was untouched by contact with the world without".

'Orme Angus' (John Charles Higginbotham), the author of *Sarah Tuldon*, lived for thirty years at North Port House, to which place he came in 1885.

St. Martin's, the Saxon Church which stands on the wall at the northern entrance to the town is the most interesting of Wareham's three churches. It is supposed to have been built in the 8th century by Aldhelm, Bishop of Sherborne, and also claims to be the burial place of Betric, King of the West Saxons. It can now lay claim to a new distinction in that it has become the shrine of Lawrence of Arabia.

After three years spent in a glorious campaign among the Arabs, Lawrence chose this corner of Dorset to indulge that part of his nature which was mystical and remote. He made his home in the lonely cottage at Moreton, near Wareham, known as 'Cloud's Hill' and spent his days there as a writer, producing some of the finest prose in our literature. His *Seven Pillars of Wisdom* and his *Letters* are recognised as classics.

Lawrence loved this part of the country and was a devotee of Thomas Hardy, whom he frequently visited at 'Max Gate'. He abhorred the vicinity of the Tank Corps at Bovington, for to him it was a desecration of the Dorset countryside.

Lawrence loved too, the little Saxon Church on the Wall at Wareham but when he knew it, it was almost in ruins. Since that time it has been restored and a fresco of the patron saint of the Church has been exposed, showing St. Martin sharing his cloak with a beggar. This is symbolic, too, of Lawrence's selfless devotion to the Arabs and makes the Church a fitting resting place for his beautifully carved effigy. This memorial was sculptured and presented to Wareham by Lawrence's friend, Eric Kennington, so that to-day the town is not only honoured on account of its age, but has become a place of pilgrimage.

THE VILLAGE OF HORTON

It is, perhaps, on account of its remoteness, that the village of Horton has not been given the prominence which is its due. This village lies one mile east of the Wimborne—Cranborne road and midway between these towns. The name Horton is of Saxon origin, (Hor—(miry or marshy) and ton—(a settlement)). Little, however, now remains as a relic of that period except a copy of the description of the settlement recorded in Domesday Book.

The Church, the stone-work of which is now covered over with Georgian brick, has a tower like an oast-house, and was built in 1401 on the site of a Benedictine Priory. The latter was founded in 961 by Orgar, the Saxon Earl of Devon. The Church has been twice rebuilt and once restored and is the only one in the country named after Wolfrida, one time Abbess of the Benedictine Priory. Underground passages have been discovered nearby which were probably made by the monks.

There are two remarkable effigies in the Church which belong to the period of the latter half of the thirteenth century. One, in Purbeck marble, is a knight, Sir Giles de Braose and the other in Ham Hill stone, a lady, supposedly Beatrice, first wife of Sir Giles.

The knight is a fine example of the Purbeck marbler's work and like all figures of knights of this period is grasping the hilt of his sword, in this case in the act of drawing it from its scabbard. He is clad in chainmail and surcoat ; his legs crossed and resting on what appears to be a lion, his head on a cushion.

The lady, belonging to the same period, is carved by a different hand. Unfortunately, much of the detail of this figure is lost but enough remains to show that she is wearing the veil and wimple worn by gentlewomen of the period. Her head rests on a cushion and her feet on a pair of lap-dogs with long tails. Unlike the Knight, her hands are folded in prayer.

On the south side of the altar there is an interesting wall monument to "Miss Lucy Uvedale, aged 6 years and 9 months", erected by her "dear Aunt, Mrs. Lucy Uvedale, who lies buried in the chancel".

This stone, together with many other monuments to the Uvedale family, were missing for some time from the church. This particular stone was found face downwards in the dairy of the Vicarage.

In the belfry, which is now the vestry, may be seen the monument to Sir Henry Hastings, son of the Earl of Huntingdon, the eccentric hunting squire who died at the age of ninety-nine. He devoted his life to sport and gave up every day to the chase. He harboured hawks and hounds, cats and dogs and was hospitable to rich and poor alike, though he himself lived upon the cheapest of foods from his own ponds and farms. It is said that, like Robin Hood, he always appeared clad in green.

The Vicarage was originally the stable and coach-house attached to Horton Manor House. These buildings were later used as a farmhouse till in 1918 the latter became the Horton Vicarage. The front, originally gabled but now plain Georgian, overlooks the valley where Sturt's lake was constructed. The brickwork of the archways under which ran the canal feeding the lake from a spring higher up the valley, is still visible.

On the hill above the village stands the look-out tower, built in 1700 by Humphrey Sturt, son of Sir Anthony Sturt, who bought the Manor of Horton from the Uvedale family in 1697. The roof of the tower was originally a cupola but has now fallen away. This observatory, built primarily to locate the herds of deer in the surrounding forest, and also the artificial lake covering 280 acres constructed at the same time are both an indication of the style peculiar to the period of landscape gardening, which Sturt evidently had in mind.

The removal of the Uvedale monuments from Horton Church is attributed to Humphrey Sturt. Why he should have done so is difficult to imagine unless it was that a disagreement between the families had arisen over the fact that one of Sturt's immediate neighbours had discovered a connection between his father and the Phoenix Brewhouse near Aldgate. (Anthony Sturt had presented a petition in 1694 setting forth that he and others were partners with Sir John Friend "in shares with the Brewhouse called the Phoenix, without Aldgate".)

By the side of the Horton plantation, north of the Ringwood—Shaftesbury road and on the border of the parish stands an ash tree which marks the spot where the Duke of Monmouth, son of Charles II, was captured in the reign of James I.

A reward of £5,000 had been offered for Monmouth's body, alive or dead. In consequence the whole country joined in the search. Monmouth, when James had succeeded to the throne, had invaded the country at Lyme Regis and gathering together a following of untrained supporters had marched into Somerset where he was defeated at Sedgemoor. He fled to Bristol and from there to Shepton Mallet, then on to Shaftesbury through Cranborne Chase to Woodyates. Here, Monmouth and two other companions left their horses, disguised themselves and endeavoured to reach Poole on foot.

It was however in the parish of Horton that all three were finally tracked down. A search of fields and ditches had been set up and the Duke's two companions were first captured. Then in a deep ditch near by, clad in shepherd's clothing, weary and faint with hunger, Monmouth himself was discovered, in his pocket a handful of raw peas, together with the badge of the Order of the Garter, indicative of his forlorn hope to gain the throne.

A week after this Monmouth was beheaded. He faced death bravely. Although, perhaps, he made a poor leader for the Protestant cause, he nevertheless did not deserve the cruel fate which was meted out to him.

The ash tree, now known as 'Monmouth's Ash', is not the original tree which grew by the ditch where he was captured, but one which has been planted in its place.

The Duke's gold snuff-box was afterwards found in the field where he was captured and handed to Mrs. Uvedale of Horton.

The old coaching inn on the Wimborne road is worthy of mention. When in the hands of the late landlord, the place was held intact as it had been for many generations. It was an eighteenth century piece, complete with oak-chest, crinolines and shawls, sporting prints, settles, open hearths and fire-irons. It was visited by dukes and duchesses, lords and ladies and journalists who came to view this incredible and complete survival of the past.

There was an interesting discovery made in a meadow at Horton in June 1875. Some boys, who were playing in a stream on the north side of the field came across a small vase and thirty or forty coins lying in the bed of the stream. The news spreading, more searches were made and more coins and vessels discovered, also an iron lance, a spear-head, a disc of bronze and some flint flakes.

Here then is concrete evidence of the ancient custom of making votive offerings to the presiding goddess of the water at the spring. Here in this very spot in the far-distant past primitive man offered his handiwork and his wealth to the giver of the waters.

It is also of interest to note that in the year 1763, Gibbon visited Horton and stayed with Humphrey Sturt at the Manor. The former records in his journal, "From this place to Mr. Sturt's, where we saw an artificial piece of water of two hundred acres, and an elegant turret a hundred and forty foot high; but such is the character of the man, that he keeps his place in no order, sells his fish and makes a granary of his turret".

It is the family of Uvedale which has its roots to this day in the village of Horton; just as the Turberville family survives in old John Durbeyfield of Hardy's novel, so the family name of Uvedale is recognised in its corruption, Udal, which is common to this day among the villagers of Horton and Holt.

THE VILLAGE OF SPETISBURY

Spetisbury is one long street lined on either side with a cosmopolitan array of houses and cottages, running parallel with the Somerset and Dorset railway. It is situated about three miles from Blandford amidst the typically wooded scenery of Dorset and close to the ancient hill known as The Hill of Yaffies or Green Woodpeckers.

It was, in fact, from the ancient earthwork, now known as Crawford Castle, on a spur of this hill that Spetisbury derived its name, 'Bury' meaning fort or earthwork and 'Spetis' in all probability from the Latin 'Spectis' meaning 'Look-out'.

The original significance of the place was this British earthwork on the southern extremity of the village built to command a full view of the surrounding forts of Dudsbury, Chalbury, Badbury, and Busbury.

It was not, however, till in 1851, when a portion of the earthwork and the Down below it was cut through in the construction of the Somerset and Dorset railway, that the magnitude of the Fort was revealed. A pit or grave was unearthed containing eighty to ninety skeletons thought to be either those of Roman soldiers or Saxon serfs. There were also the weapons which were buried with them, iron spear-heads, blades, swords, spears and arrow-heads. There was a javelin 10 inches long, a cauldron with two handles, a colander, some pottery, a bone comb five inches in length, and iron and bone pins and needles.

Spetisbury, although now a busy thoroughfare, has somehow maintained its rustic atmosphere and the Halt, somewhat difficult of access, overlooking its long street, gives it an air of quaint distinction.

Like most Dorset villages, too, it has its local Folk Lore. The old natives of Spetisbury will tell you that before ever Bland, ford was built, there on the Downs between Spetisbury and Charlton, stood the City of Bland, and that you can see to this day-the shapes of its streets marked on the Downs. There was also an inn, they say, which stood long after the City had gone, called the 'Rendez-vous' but known to the villagers as the 'Randy-booze'.

An old Spetisbury farmer says there was once a prison camp for French soldiers during the Napoleonic Wars on the site of the ancient city and he adds, "They d'zay that when the people were diggin' out an' makin' up Badbury Rings and Castle Rings there were only one pick an' shovel between 'em, zoo they did pass the tools back an' for'ard, when oone were pickin' t'other were shovellin'."

Among the last of the buildings which line the village street we come, as the road proceeds to Charlton Marshall to the Church on the left and the old and the new Rectory on the right.

The Church, which is 13th century, was restored during the middle of the last Century. The solid square tower and the three graceful pillars are the only remaining part of the original structure. The old style has been carefully retained, both within and without the building, using the old material. The exterior of the Church has a beauty of its own which shows to best advantage in the mellow light of a September morning when the embedded flint catches the rays of the sun and sparkles like precious stones.

The pulpit, which is of the period of James I, is beautifully carved and has above it an hour-glass, in perfect preservation.

Other items of interest in this little wayside church are a chained copy of Archbishop Jewell's Apology of the 17th century, and Bowyer's ancient tomb with its canopy of stone (1599).

The Communion Plate has been carefully preserved. Some of the vessels were given by a former and noted Rector, Dr. Charles Sloper in 1727.

Opposite the door of the church is the curious pyramid-shaped tomb of the Rev. Thomas Rackett, another well-known Rector of Spetisbury (1780-1840).

The old Rectory on the opposite side of the street is a stately building rich in historical interest. It is a Queen Anne house with Georgian windows and porch, erected in 1716 by Dr. Charles Sloper, Chancellor of the Diocese and Rector of Spetisbury and Charlton Marshall. Dr. Sloper also built Charlton Church and endowed the Spetisbury schools. The old Rectory, or John's House, as it is now called, was built on top of a Jacobean Rectory which still remains in the basement. At the south end clay walls, and nearby a very old well faced with knapped flint indicate the existence of an ancient Dorset dwelling probably dating from 1200.

It is then obvious that the house was enlarged in Jacobean times before it was built over by Dr. Sloper in Queen Anne style. The front of the house with its decorated roof-surround and classical head of Wisdom in the centre is typical of the period. The garden front overlooking smooth lawns adorned with fine old trees, is particularly delightful, having steps with massive stone balusters beautifully panelled. The upper Queen Anne windows with their heavy woodwork are here easily distinguished from the leaded Jacobean windows below.

The interior of the house is, of course, mainly in Queen Anne style. The hall, entered by a pillared porch, with a fanlight of fine workmanship over the door, is impressively beautiful with its dark Jacobean furniture, oak panelling and polished stone floor. The walls above the panelling now show their original duck-egg green paint of 1716.

The oak panelling and shaped balusters of the staircase are of great beauty and dignity. The large Queen Anne window at the top runs up on its sash at a touch.

The landing is perfectly proportioned and the doors well spaced. The hall, staircase and landing are, in fact, all examples of the superb architecture of the period.

An interesting exposure was made in 1945, when in a process of reconstruction, a roof-beam, like a tree with its branches lopped off, was found under the landing floor. This was the original 'roof tree' of the old Jacobean rectory.

It was during the tenancy of the Rev. Thomas Racket that illustrious visitors frequented the Old Rectory. David Garrick, the actor, was one of these, also Sheridan, the playwright, and George Romney, the artist. The latter painted Thomas Rackett, his wife and son. It is thought highly probable that both Rackett and his son were painted at the house. In a cupboard, close to the garden doorway, are smears of red and green oil colours on the wall. These colours are identical with those used in Romney's portrait of the young Rackett against a background of green nut trees. It is a fascinating conjecture that Romney kept his paints in this very cupboard and that he cleaned his brushes on the wall.

The picture of young Thomas in his red coat, buff breeches, buckled shoes, grey stockings and cocked hat lying on the ground, also that of the Rev. Thomas in black coat and pale-blue frilled waistcoat are delightful souvenirs of Romney's visits to Spetisbury.

Thomas Rackett himself was a keen botanist, a great collector of china and minerals, and a connoisseur of art. Without a doubt he planted the Fern-leaf beech, walnuts and hornbeams on the Rectory lawns.

Some little distance away, on the same side of the road, we find an old thatched cottage, now a roadside cafe. This is a combination of two old labourer's dwellings known to-day as 'Marigold Cottage'. The thatched roof, low ceilings, oak beams, immensely thick walls and wide fireplaces indicate a 16th century dwelling place. Other old thatched cottages, possibly of the same period on the side of the road near the railway, have been gradually burnt to the ground by fire from the trains, leaving 'Marigold Cottage' the distinction of being the oldest in the village.

It would seem, then, that Spetisbury, which sprang into being so long ago at the foot of a hill-fortress might lay claim to be one of the most ancient of Dorset villages, its long winding street leading once to the City of Bland, but to-day to the thriving market town of Blandford-Forum.

BERE REGIS

Bere Regis, situated six miles to the north-east of Wareham, is one of the most interesting of small Dorset towns on account of its Royal association with Saxon times, the architecture of its church and the one-time glory of the annual Fair on Woodbury Hill.

There have been various suggestions as to the origin of its name. No doubt the story that King John was so delighted with the beer of which he drank during his sojourn in the town that he declared its name should be Beer for ever more is false. Unlikely, too, is the supposition that "Bere", the Hebrew for 'well', is connected with the place. It is far more feasible that the name is derived from the Scandinavian word 'bere' which means a cluster of buildings or farmstead and survives in the words 'borough', 'bury', and 'by'.

Hutchins derives the name from a word meaning 'low, scrubby wood', and even to-day Bere Regis is still well wooded and the trees in the neighbouring village of Bloxworth are some of the most beautiful in the county. It is of interest to note that William Barnes, the Dorset poet, held this view of the origin of the name of Bere Regis.

The town's first association with royalty was in the days of the Saxon Queen Elfrida who, in 979, fled from Corfe Castle here when suspicion was cast upon her for the murder of her stepson, Edward the Martyr. Here, too, Ethelred, the brother of the murdered boy, who now inherited the throne, is reported to have been beaten by his mother with big wax candles when he wept for the death of his brother. For this reason, it is chronicled, "Ethelred ever hated wax candles, and would not have them burnt before him all the days of his life".

In 1205 King John came to reside at Bere—after having given up an attempt to invade the coasts of Normandy. He built a castle here and erected a kitchen for his service and it is thought a possibility that from moneys extracted from his subjects he helped to build the church. Of this, however, there is no proof, but there is a crowned and bearded head on the westernmost pier of the church which could be that of the dissolute monarch, and also he is known to have ordered "a fair crucifix to be set up in our Chapel at Bere".

After the residency of King John the manor passed into the hands of the Abbess of Tarent. It consisted at that time of 'a fair, a market, a free warren, and the whole forest of Bere". Many of the abbesses were buried here and the last of them, Margaret Russell, requested in her will (1567) that she should be buried in the church of Bere.

Most of the church was erected, in all probability, during the time of its connection with the Abbey of Tarent in the fourteenth and fifteenth centuries.

Simon de Montfort, the founder of the English Parliament was associated with Bere Regis and later the Turbervilles who came over with the Conqueror, made this their headquarters.

The Turbervilles were a noted family well established in the West Country by the end of the 12th century. They held manors in various places, but that of Bere Regis was the most important. Their mansion here was destroyed, but a drawing was preserved, an engraving from which is still in existence.

Several members of the family were outstanding. Henry Turberville, in the reign of King John and Henry III obtained military glory; James Turberville, who was born at Bere, became, in the reign of Mary Tudor, Bishop of Exeter. He was a strong Roman Catholic, and refusing to take the oath to a Protestant sovereign, was thrown into the Tower.

George Turberville, born at Winterborne Whitchurch, was an Elizabethan poet of some consequence although he is now forgotten.

The Turberville tombs are to be found in the south aisle of the church and their arms on the windows above.

There is a story told that one of the Turberville squires quarrelled with the Vicar of the time and vowed he would never enter the church doors again. Eventually, however, his anger cooled and the Lord of the Manor had a doorway cut through one of the arches, that he might enter the church without breaking his word.

Their family name survives to this day in various forms amongst the peasant stock of the neighbourhood.

It was from the corruption 'Durberfield' that Hardy based the theme of Tess whose humble family owed its origin to the Turbervilles of 'King's Bere'.

It is also generally supposed that the 'Barleigh' of Orme Angus's novel, *Sarah Tuldon* is Bere Regis.

So this little town is marked out by literary fame and can claim a Royal patronage but to-day, the only remaining evidence of its former glories (for its annual fair has dwindled almost to nothing), is its church.

This 15th century building has been conscientiously restored. One arcade is Norman, also the font which has been preserved intact. There are two beautifully carved medieval seat-ends opposite the porch door and inside the porch two iron fire-hooks, relics from the days when they were used to pull the thatch from a burning roof.

There is a monument in the Chancel in the form of a kneeling Tudor couple facing each other. The woman is Margaret Skerne of the old Spanish family of Skerne. She apparently was responsible for the quaint lines engraved on the tomb in 1596:

"If each thing cude doe each thing's worth expresse,
What is man's life but vain unperfectness?
How swiftlie rune we to our fatall ende,
Which have no hope if death be not our frende!
I Skerne, doe show that all our earthlie truste,
All earthlie fayres, and goods, and sweets are dust
Look on the worldes insyde, and looke on me.
Her outside is but painted vanitie."

Around the church is a series of modern windows which depict in beautiful design the full story of the Gospel.

There are old Jacobean panels in the vestry and interesting tiles in the porch and chancel copies from those of Bindon Abbey. But it is the Nave roof which is the glory of this church of St. John the Baptist, and is thought to be unique.

It is said to have been built by Cardinal Moreton whilst he was Archbishop of Canterbury and after he was instrumental in bringing about a reconciliation during the Wars of the Roses. Besides bearing the Moreton Arms and the Cardinal himself, the central bosses of the roof show the Tudor Rose indicating Moreton's share in promoting peace by the marriage of Elizabeth of York and Henry Tudor.

The most outstanding feature of this remarkable roof is the termination of the hammer-beams in quaint projecting figures dressed in 15th century costumes thought at one time to represent the twelve Apostles. The underside of the easternmost tie-beam bears the head of St. John the Baptist.

In 1785 the roof was restored and the timbers repainted and gilded by an artist with some conception of Italian art. The effect is striking, if somewhat crude.

Cardinal Moreton also built the tower which has six bells, the oldest of which was cast in Cromwell's time and the last addition in 1919 bearing the word 'Pax'.

The Cardinal was born near Bere Regis and was at one time Rector of Bloxworth. He evidently held the Church in much affection and esteem. In his will he left money for a priest to say mass in Bere Church for his departed soul.

LATE SPRING

The blackthorn be white on the hedgerow now,
The cuckoo d' call clear an' bold,
The sky be s'blue o'er the green o' the vields
Where the buddercups vlourish their gold.

The blossom be out on the orchard bough,
The chestnut tree be in vlower,
The bluebells be thick in the shady woods
Along be the zide o' the Stour.

The rivers an' valleys an' trees an' vields
Do all zeem to I t'be glad,
Yet while this zweet zight my eyes do behold,
'Tis only my heart that be sad.

SQUARE & COMPASS, WORTH MATRAVERS.

THE SQUARE AND COMPASS

The Square and Compass, standing at the top of the hill which leads down into the village of Worth Matravers, near Swanage, is one of the oldest of Dorset inns. Like the rest of the dwellings in this area it is built entirely of stone hewn from the nearby quarries. Without showing any signs of defacement this little inn has weathered five centuries of exposure to storm and gale, for Worth stands only a mile from the coast and has many a tale to tell of shipwreck and disaster. In the vestry of the church which is older still than the inn, hangs a mirror reclaimed from the wreck of the *Halswell* in 1786 when she struck the rocks and was completely destroyed.

The exterior of the Square and Compass presents an inviting appearance despite its rather bare frontage. The quaint little porch is formed by two complete slabs of stone on either side, the top overgrown by flowering plants which give a picturesque effect. A long low wall runs along the outside of the inn proving an ideal resting place for tankards of ale, or mugs of beer and providing a seat on summer evenings for the worthies who frequent this friendly establishment.

There is no doubt that the Square and Compass was the scene of much activity during the days of smuggling. It commands a wide view of the Purbeck Downs and might well have served as a look-out for the Preventive Officers of the illicit trade.

For many years it has been the resort of artists and has been made famous by the frequent visits of Augustus John who, whilst he lived at Ferndown, near Wimborne, was a frequent visitor at the inn. Many of his sketches adorn the walls, among them a drawing of the late lamented host, Mr. Charles Newman. There is also a portrait of Augustus John by Low.

Mr. Newman was a Dorset man and a genial soul who knew and loved the Dorset countryside. His personality still lingers in the place. You see him photographed with Leslie Bankes, the film star, holding aloft a mug of ale wearing a smile which made him the ideal host. You see him again standing before the T.V. camera, when, quite recently, he gave a talk about the quarries he knew so well.

Once more in the Tap Room he looks down from the walls, this time depicted by a cartoonist as a gigantic figure pursuing a dog. His countenance is determined but even in this caricature the kindly humour of the man is apparent to the observant.

Other paintings and sketches hang on the walls, among them a water-colour of Winspit, the cave nearer the village of Worth. A steep descent leads down to the cave but the traveller is rewarded by the unexpected beauty of this sheltered little bay. Perhaps on account of its inaccessibility it is unfrequented and has not been commercialised. It lies undisturbed and peaceful, its natural contours but little altered since the Normans invaded our shores.

Sculptures, too, have found their way to this old-world inn, for leaning against the wall outside are to be seen engravings in Purbeck stone of the Aga Khan, his horse Mahmoud, and the friendly host himself.

Standing outside the inn it is easy to see why this little place has been for so many years the paradise of artists for there before you stretches the purple and brown heath, the contours of which have changed only with the seasons through the centuries and in the distance the Purbeck Hills forming a natural background to this unspoilt countryside.

The view of the Purbecks from this point is particularly interesting for the ridges still discernable on the hillside are thought to be the outline of cultivation terraces marked out in Saxon times.

Step inside the inn and you soon discover that the welcome this place has always given is still to be found to-day for Mr. Newman's widow carries on its tradition of good fellowship and cheer.

There in the 'Dining Room,' besides the painting and sketches, hangs the Dart Board and in the tiny Tap Room a cheerful fire burns. There are no signs of disrepair, only the low ceilings and thick walls give any indication of the age of the building.

It was close on fifty years ago when the Newmans first took over the Square and Compass. Then part of the dining room was a stable with a cobbled floor. This being no longer necessary

SMITH'S ARMS, GODMANSTONE.

the cobbles were unearthed and that portion of the building added to the smaller apartment to make the long room we see to-day.

The Inn-sign bears the name only, on a board fixed to a post reminding us, perhaps, of the long-ago days when the Steward and Jury of Bridport in 1593 ordered that all those who kept 'tipling' in the borough should set out an Ale Stake or Ale Pole "during such time as they have drink to sell". Before this a bush of ivy had been fixed to the end of the pole as a sign for an Ale House, but now it was decided that "Good wine needed no bush" or that "Acceptable wine was not in need of Ivy".

The plain lettering used for the sign of "The Square and Compass" is typical of the single-mindedness of the villagers who have quarried their local stone since the Norman invasion.

The square and compass are the tools used in the measurement of the stone for the purpose of building and it is only fitting that this little inn where the quarrymen foregathered in their leisure hours should bear the sign of their trade.

They are proud to tell you that a large portion of the marble used in the construction of Salisbury Cathedral was hewn from the quarries of Downshay, in the village of Worth, and given for that purpose by a former Lady of the Manor.

Come to the 'Square and Compass' expecting luxury and ultra-modern convenience and you will be disappointed, but seek cleanliness, warmth, good fellowship and cheer and you will not look in vain.

DORSET'S SMALLEST INN

The Smith's Arms, Godmanstone

The Smith's Arms is to be found in the little village of Godmanstone, five miles from Dorchester. It claims to be the smallest inn in England, and there seems little evidence to doubt its claim for its diminutive bar measures 20 ft. by 11 ft. and on one occasion when it held 75 people, that number was its full capacity.

This little erection nestles at the foot of Cowdon Hill and by its side flows the River Cerne. The inn presents a rustic and intriguing appearance, having a conical-shaped thatched roof and an inviting little porch with a carriage lantern on either side. The inn-sign which has been recently reproduced by a Bridport artist, shows the blacksmith at his forge, a pair of pincers and a red-hot horse-shoe in one hand, and a hammer in the other. This style of inn-sign is a relic of days long past when a painted sign was set up outside a building to denote the trade carried on within. Very few of the ordinary folk then could read or write but a picture could be understood by all.

Four hundred years ago this little building was a smithy. What is now the cellar was originally the forge and the horses were shod in the bar. The large fireplace may still be seen. The walls, which are very thick are made of dried mud and flint, the ceiling is low and sloping. The place is in extremely good repair but the old-world atmosphere has been carefully preserved by lanterns hanging from the ceiling and brasses for ornamentation.

This little inn boasts a legend and is visited, I am told, from all over the world. Two years ago the Minister of Agriculture from Australia, when staying at Wimborne came to see this unique establishment, for Mr. and Mrs. Len Arnold, who have been host and hostess here for eight years, declare it to be the only one-bar lock-up, fully licensed house in the world. Each night after Mr. and Mrs. Arnold have served their last customer, they lock up outside and go to their home near-by. Although so very small, this tiny inn yields quite good dividends, for, by reason of its quaint charm and air of hospitality it draws outside as well as local patronage.

According to the legend which is printed beneath the inn-sign over the porch, King Charles II when travelling the south-west of England, 300 years ago, stopped his carriage outside this small smithy at Godmanstone to have his horses shod. At the same time, his Majesty desired a drink, so requested the blacksmith to send him out a glass of ale. "I have no licence, sire," the smith replied. So there and then, the King, thinking it a suitable place for refreshment by the wayside, granted him one.

Upon this, the blacksmith had a bar set up in front of the smithy. He continued to shoe horses but sold ale at the same time, and after its Royal patronage, there is no doubt that it became the most popular blacksmith's shop in the West Country.

The exact date when the last horse was shod here does not seem to have been recorded, but the place, no doubt, fell into disuse as a smithy, like many such, when cars usurped the road, but here it stands to-day, an engaging little relic right in the heart of Dorset and the Hardy country, offering, as it did to that merry monarch three hundred years ago, refreshment by the wayside in this pleasant downland village.

THE KING'S STAG INN

Whilst travelling the country roads at Kings Stag, a little Dorset village near Sturminster Newton, we came upon the framework of a large inn-sign standing by the wayside. We made enquiries concerning it and found that, till quite recently, it framed an old inn-sign—a stag with a golden collar round its neck and underneath it the printed lines :

"When Julius Caesar landed here
I was then a little deer ;
When Julius Caesar reigned King
Round my neck they put this ring.
Whoever shall me overtake,
Save my life for Caesar's sake."

Unfortunately the sign was taken down and placed in a nearby shed as callers invaded the house opposite, taking it to be the place the sign indicated. We could see the sign leaning against the wall, of the shed and could just distinguish some of the words in the last line of the verse.

This old sign originally belonged to the King's Stag Inn which once stood near the bridge of that name leading into the village.

The bridge, and consequently the inn and village, derived its name from an ancient legend concerning the King's deer during the reign of Henry III. The Vale of Blackmore was the king's favourite hunting ground for the famous white deer of the district.

He is said to have spared the life of a beautiful white hart which, however, was later killed in the chase by a nobleman, de la Linde, close by the bridge. The King was indignant, and not only imprisoned and fined the nobleman but placed a permanent tax upon his lands which money was known as White Hart Silver and gave the Blackmore Vale the name of "Whiteharte Forest". The De la Linde family afterwards adopted as their coat of arms, white hart heads on a red shield.

To this day the village of Kings Stag is proud of its light-coloured deer which are to be seen in the grounds of Stock House, the seat of the Yeatman family. The villagers will tell you that a black deer once strayed, much to their consternation, among the local herd. It was quickly routed before the fair reputation of the white deer was soiled.

So this interesting old bridge which spans the Lydden brook was given the name of the stag which met its death close by.

Like so many of these old bridges in Dorset the Kings Stag bridge bears the notice of the Transportation penalty :

> "Any person wilfully injuring any part of this County Bridge will be guilty of felony and upon conviction liable to be transported for life."
>
> "By the Court."

In the case of King's Stag bridge the threat must have been effective for it is perfectly intact and extremely well preserved. Its three rounded arches, buttressed on the upstream side to break the flow of the water, appear to be as untouched as the pillars of a church. The foundation of this bridge is supposedly Roman, the remainder being of a much later date.

Sixty years ago the old inn was still standing near the bridge with its painted sign outside but was at that time completely destroyed by fire. The sign was taken down and placed in a tile-yard till, in the reign of King George VI, who was a lover of old inn-signs, interest in these relics revived, many of the discarded signs were resurrected and repainted. The King's Stag sign was consequently then removed from the tile-yard and placed higher up in the village where the frame still stands.

The verse on the sign, it will be noted, reverts to Julius Caesar. This suggests that the celebrated deer of the 'Whiteharte Forest' were to be found here before the days of Roman occupation and that Caesar himself had the same desire as his royal successor to spare the life of a beautiful deer.

This idea is not without foundation for many Roman remains have been unearthed in this district and tessalated pavements indicating the site of Roman villas. The old pack-horse bridge in the neighbouring village of Fifehead Neville claims to be Roman and we know that Caesar's emblem was a white hart.

To-day there are at least thirteen inns called 'The White Hart', either in or around the Blackmore Vale, bringing to the mind the county's pride in its heritage of local deer.

'The Green Man', a few hundred yards away from where the King's Stag inn once stood, has taken the place of the old inn.

The Green Man refers to the herbalist or quack doctor who in the old days dealt in medicinal herbs. The sign at one time showed the Green Man himself but to-day we see only the plain printed sign without any form of decoration.

The landlord here is well-versed in local lore and shares the pride of the village folk in their ancient legend of the King's favourite Stag.

THE DAMORY OAK

The Damory Oak inn which stands near the railway arches on the outskirts of Blandford has an interesting history which is closely linked to that of the town.

A little to the north of where the inn now stands there grew a gigantic oak exceeding in measurement an oak tree in America which at that time claimed to be the largest in the world. The tree in Los Angeles measured 37 ft. 4 in. round the trunk but the Blandford monster measured 68 ft. round at ground level and 23 ft. in diameter. Though during the violent storm of 1703 many of its branches had been torn off, in 1747 they extended 72 ft. across and the oak stood 75 ft. high. It was at its best during the reign of Edward III but by Cromwell's time its core had decayed and become hollow. The cavity measured 15 ft. wide and 17 ft. high and could house twenty men. During the Civil War and till after the Restoration an old man sold ale in it.

Someone has said that if this oak were still in existence Blandford would be a place of pilgrimage like Stonehenge or Glastonbury, but the tree came to a somewhat ignominious end for in 1755 it was sold for £14, rooted up and its wood sold for firing.

Fortunately there is a memorial to this famous oak for close to where it grew an inn was erected and given the name of the tree it commemorates, 'The Damory Oak'.

It was through its connection with the D'Amorie estate that the tree was so named. It grew close to Damory Court which was the seat of Roger Damory, a descendant of the D'Amorie family who were given lands by William I.

Roger Damory was the last possessor of the Manor and was a prominent figure during the reign of Edward II. He fought in the wars with Scotland, was Constable of Corfe Castle during the year 1320-1321, also Warden of the Forest of Purbeck and was summoned to Parliament as a Baron by the reigning king.

Later, however, he took part against the King with Thomas, Earl of Lancaster and died in a march into the North. He was buried in the Priory church of Ware.

Damory Court, which eventually belonged to the Ryves family, became a farm but is known to-day as the Damory Hotel and bears for its sign the Damory coat of arms, a blue hand on a red and white background.

But it is the little inn by the railway arches which perpetuates the memory of the gallant oak which after the great fire of Blandford in 1731, housed two homeless families in its hollow trunk.

The fire began on a Friday afternoon at 2 o'clock at a soap-boilers or tallow-chandlers which stood where four streets meet at the end of Salisbury Street. The stiff north-easterly wind which was blowing at the time carried the flames all over the town. Twenty houses were on fire in a quarter of an hour, and in half-an-hour three fire-engines were rendered useless. The direction of the wind then changing to northwards, the fire was carried to Blandford St. Mary and Bryanston and these two villages, with the exception of three houses, were completely destroyed.

The flames finally broke out in the roof of the Blandford

Church, melting the bells and the lead covering the spire. By this time the pumps and engines had all been destroyed and the people of the town were exhausted with fighting the fire so that no attempt was made to save the church which was completely destroyed. It was fortunate, however, that the townsfolk were able to remove the goods which had been stored in the church for safety before its final collapse.

Small-pox raged in this ill-fated town at the same time as the fire, sixty families being stricken. It will always be to the credit of those who attended the sick and removed them through fields and gardens to safety outside the town, that only one died by reason of the fire.

Altogether four hundred families were rendered homeless and it was at this time, whilst wooden barracks were being put up to house the poor, that two families took refuge in the hollow of the Damory oak tree and lived there till they had other accommodation.

Thus it is that the inn-sign depicts children playing around the hollow oak which was their home while their father looks from the doorway. Fortunately the sign is still standing for, despite the glory of its name, the inn is known to the local people as 'The Hole in the Wall', on account of beer having been at one time handed through a hole in the wall to the stables at the back. Its true name, however, survives in the name of the local Slate Club which is called the 'Damory Oak'.

After the devastation of the town only three of the original houses were left standing, the Ryves Almshouses, a German doctor's dwelling-house, known to-day as the Old House and an old barn, once part of a Leper hospital, which stands about 300 yards from the Damory Oak.

In 1732, a year after the fire King George II passed an Act to rebuild the town. His Majesty gave £1,000, the Queen £200 and the Prince of Wales £100 towards this end and so a new Blandford Forum arose including the beautiful church we see to-day, but it is this little wayside inn, The Damory Oak, which provides the most pathetic link with the tragedy of 1731.

THE BULL'S HEAD

Two inns in Poole have been recently scheduled as being of historical or architectural interest and have been added to the Protected List. These are 'The Bull's Head Inn', High Street, Poole, and 'The Malster's Arms', Lagland Street, Poole. Their interest is architectural as well as historical as both inns retain part of their original structure. The Bull's Head has the distinction, too, of being in existence when 400 years ago the first Licensing Act came into force, for on May 1st 1552, King Edward VI's Parliament made compulsory the notice above Public House doorways announcing the landlord's licence to sell drink and tobacco. The landlord was also compelled by law to sign a document whereby he was under penalty of £10 to keep the 'typlynge' house and to agree to the banning of "unlawful play at tables, dice, tennis and bowls".

The present landlord of the Bull's Head, Mr. E. P. Shorto, has delved deeply into the past history of this interesting old inn and maintains the original dignity and hospitality of the ancient hostelries whose function it was to provide people with shelter and horses with fodder.

The Bull's Head was constructed of Purbeck stone in the late 16th century as a Coaching Inn. Traces of hinges on the outside walls suggest that double gates once dignified its entrance and the deep mullioned windows of the adjoining house plus the wine-cellar below have led historians to suppose that this building once formed part of the original structure.

The wine-cellar is impressive and having descended into its cool recesses one is immediately transported into an atmosphere of bygone mystery and intrigue. How many plots have been engendered inside these thick stone walls ! How often have smugglers hidden here their contraband goods stealthily unloaded so close at hand !

The massive overhead beams are of solid oak and the walls 3 ft. 6 in. in width, but despite its ancient construction and atmosphere this wine-cellar is fitted up with every modern contrivance. There is telescopic piping attached to the barrels and a beer-engine which, in perfect working order, contrives to maintain a temperature of 55°F. This keeps the beer in good condition and makes it possible for Mr. Shorto to hand to his customers at all times a clear and palatable drink.

It is, however, the ceiling of a first-floor room, originally 21 ft. by 20 ft. but since sub-divided, which is the gem of the whole building. It is of modelled plaster and with the adjoining frieze has been perfectly preserved from the late-Tudor date when it was designed and fashioned by unknown hands. The pattern of the ceiling which is based on the square and circle, is of a remarkable beauty, enhanced by the fact that it was not precast but moulded by the skilful hands of the nameless craftsman. In two places the pattern stops abruptly. Does this mean that the artist died before his work was completed and that here, in the Bull's Head, Poole, we have yet another 'Unfinished Symphony', preserved through the centuries?

On the ground floor, in what is now the Saloon Bar, may be seen the eight-foot chimney of an original fireplace. It is, however, partially hidden by modern brickwork.

It is of great interest to note that the late Borough historian, Mr. H. P. Smith, M.B.E., discovered many entries of meetings held at the Bull's Head during the 17th and 18th centuries. It seems that the Poole City Fathers preferred to meet here rather than in the draughty Guildhall, then in Fish Street. The wine, beer and tobacco consumed at the meetings were paid for by the Corporation and among many interesting entries we find :

"Oct. 20th, 1715.

"Paid for 19 Bottles of wine drunk in ye walke on ye King's Coronation Day £1/8/6.

"Paid at Bull's Head for beare for Gunners 2/6."

The 'walke' was the open space in front of the Town Cellars and Harbour Office. The occasion was the celebration of the suppression of the Jacobite Rebellion in 1715.

The Gunners were called in to fire a salute and thus later were included in the rejoicings held at the Bull's Head.

The sign outside the inn to-day is comparatively modern. The previous one depicted a somewhat gory bull's head, com-

THE
WORLD'S END
INN

pletely severed from the body, looking ferociously through an archway. The effect was crude but perhaps more startling than the present decorous painting suspended from the frontage of the inn.

Poole may be justly proud of its two 'Protected Inns' and glad to know that they will be preserved as Ancient Monuments of the Borough.

Mr. Shorto, who has been landlord of the Bull's Head for close on 17 years evidently regards the place as his own particular 'Trust House'. He has most carefully refrained from the violation of any of the laws set down in the first Licensing Acts of 1552.

He makes the spacious cellar his workshop. Here in the atmosphere of a bygone age he spends many of his leisure hours. He has made such a close study of these ancient vaults that one day I am sure he will stumble upon the information he is looking for to fill the gaps still left in the history of this inn.

I shall not forget the pride with which Mr. Shorto, by wielding an axe, exhibited the texture of the massive oak beams of the cellar floor. Neither shall I forget the reverence with which he showed me the magnificent moulding of the Elizabethan ceiling.

Everywhere he has maintained with loving care the atmosphere of this ancient inn. The old mahogany clock, standing on the landing, probably 17th century, is a museum piece of the landlord's own collection. In fact, Mr. Shorto's pride in this inn to which he is entrusted equals that bestowed by some ancient lineage on their ancestral mansions.

WORLD'S END

As the name suggests the quaint old inn, 'World's End' is to to be found in a remote part of Dorset, where, it is commonly supposed, four parishes meet, and the boundary line of Wareham and Wimborne runs through the building.

This long, low thatched dwelling is half inn and half farm, and is situated in the parish of Almer and about a mile from the village of Morden. The actual date of its erection is not known but it was one of the first inns in the county to be licensed.

Everything in this fascinating old building is in miniature. The tiny bar-parlour is capable of seating hardly more than twenty people but what strikes one as most remarkable about this place is that, although the rooms are so small, three parts of the population of the world must, at some time or other, have visited this inn, for every available space on walls and ceiling, not only in this room, but in the other two belonging to the inn, is covered with signatures. These signatures appear to be of people of all nationalities.

Among the vast number of names on the ceiling of the bar-parlour alone there were Irish, Scottish, Belgian, Dutch, Italian, and German, besides the names of various ships, the owers of whose signatures must at some time have sat in this little old inn. One receives the impression that it would be no less impossible to count the number of stars in our universe than the names inscribed on the ceiling and walls of this dwelling.

The bar-parlour is complete in its old-world setting, there is the old-fashioned fireplace with its piled-up logs ! There on either side of it are the inviting ingle-nooks. To the left of the fireplace is the bread-oven in the wall and to the right the high-backed oak settle to keep out the draughts and another one opposite facing the fire.

Gone, however, is the oil lamp once suspended from the oaken beam on the low ceiling. The busy landlord's wife has her hands already full with the farm as well as the inn and must avail herself of the benefits of some economy of labour. The floor is still covered with flag-stones which must take a deal of scrubbing.

The dart-board is extremely well worn especially on its outer edges. It would appear that more often than not the target has been missed. Does that mean that this out-of-the-world inn provides more potent drinks !

It was here in this little bar-parlour, I was told, that long ago the 'regulars' used to perform a brush-dance for their own amusement with a fiddle to supply the music, two of the men would take it in turns to side-step an old-fashioned broom in time to the music, then throwing the broom to his partner he repeated the action and returned the broom. This was done with such agility and dexterity, no doubt to some good old Dorset tune, that it must have been an entertaining spectacle indeed.

'World's End' proudly calls one small apartment 'Monty's Room' for in 1942 General Montgomery stayed in this inn. The people of the village like to think that here in the seclusion of this quiet spot the great man planned out his campaign for the invasion of Normandy. I have never heard that the landlord's wife asked him to give an eye to the cakes in the oven ! If so, I've no doubt he would, like Alfred the Great, have let them burn, for posterity to commemorate, not only at World's End, but all over the country !

'Monty', like every other visitor, has written his name on the wall of the room, but sad to say, some anti-militarist has tried to erase it.

The other room in the inn is called the Signature Room, for indeed it could be called nothing else. There is scarcely room for a pin's head between the signatures, some indeed are on top of the other. It is truly an amazing spectacle. Young and old have signed their names and here and there stands out the age-old sign of a lover's tryst, two hearts joined by Cupid's dart, and the lovers' names inscribed.

Leading from the bar-parlour is the 'cellar'. This is now used as the bar. There are iron hooks suspended from the ceiling and these, I am told, are relics of the time when a butcher kept the inn and hung his sides of meat on the hooks.

The cellar leads into the dairy which was rebuilt at a comparatively recent date and this leads into what was once the stable where the stage coaches changed horses, for this was originally a coaching inn on what was then the main road from London to Exeter.

At the end of this long building is the stable which is in use to-day and at right-angles to this the bar. Here and also in the middle part of the house the original timber still remains. During the reconstruction of part of the house the rafters, when removed, crumbled into powder, giving some idea of the ancient structure of the building.

The exterior of the house rather belies its significance for outside there is nothing to distinguish it from an ordinary cottage except the name over the small door and the tall inn-sign. The house stands a little way back from the road and here on a summer evening the long stretch of the house is lined with cars upon the occupants of which mine host attends in person.

There is then a stir of life in this quiet spot. Folks, differently clad and differently conveyed, come showing much the same spirit as did those guests of long ago, when the wheels of the stage-coach rumbled up and my lord called for a drink and my lady stepped lightly from her carriage holding up her voluminous skirts.

'World's End' is appropriately named on account of its isolation, but must have proved a happy journey's end to many a weary traveller for this little inn still gives to all who call a friendly smile of welcome and a parting word of cheer.

LITTLE TALES

MISS BILLETT'S FORTUNE

Until the night Miss Billett died, the little drama daily enacted in her cottage remained a mystery. All the village except those immediately concerned, wondered how it was that Miss Billett, for close on twenty years, had never lacked a helper. She had but to breathe a request and her little band of followers rushed to do her bidding. Indeed, in her latter years, Miss Billett did nothing in the nature of housework at all, save make known her wishes to her ready helpers.

An aura of mystery surrounded Miss Billett. She wore her lace cap with becoming dignity. She alluded sometimes, but not too frequently, to her wealthy connections. These allusions were vague enough to be tantalizing, so that the supposition soon came to be regarded as fact, and news spread over the village that Miss Billett had close relatives who were worth their thousands.

That explained, of course, why the old lady's cottage contained such valuable pieces of furniture. Miss Billett, herself, never explained them but she saw to it that all her helpers kept them free from dust and well polished.

In front of her cottage lay a little patch of garden where never a weed was to be seen, where in season the bright flowers bloomed and roses twined around the door.

Miss Billett had never been known to do any gardening herself, but at those times of the year when gardens need most attention, there could be seen the husband of one of her helpmates, working as if his very life depended upon it in Miss Billett's garden.

It was almost pathetic to witness the solicitude of her faithfuls when Miss Billett suffered any ailment, whether a cold in the head, a chill, or one of her frequent attacks of bronchitis. One after another they came, with over-anxious faces, bearing perhaps a milk pudding to tempt her appetite, or some embrocation for her chest, and each offered willing service at any hour of night or day.

How other lonely souls of the village envied Miss Billett! What, they wondered, could be the secret of her spell. It had somehow leaked out that not one of Miss Billett's obligers received a penny for their trouble yet they laboured with a zeal almost fanatic.

How the clear window-panes of the old lady's cottage caught the morning light and reflected the rays of the setting sun! How spotless was Miss Billett's door-step, how fresh the well-watered geraniums that bloomed on her window-bench!

It was surprising, most people thought, that Miss Billett had never married as, obviously, she could charm. After much consideration, they decided that Miss Billett's single state must have been from choice. It was well known that at least once when she lived in the next village she had been on the verge of matrimony, for she had walked out with the stalwart young village blacksmith; and a handsome pair they had made. Miss Billett had been pretty, in fact she still was, with her pink cheeks and silver hair, though now her face had hardened and she wore an air of perpetual reserve.

Whilst courting, the blacksmith had given her a pair of fire tongs which he had forged with his own hands, thereby proving that his attentions were honourable, and showed that he hoped to spend years of domestic bliss with Miss Billett by his side. However, this state never materialised, but Miss Billett kept the tongs, and no-one ever quite knew what had happened.

As the years went by Miss Billett became more and more mysterious. She did not completely open her heart to anyone, and no one, as was customary in the village, called her by her Christian name. She was Miss Billett to everyone till her dying day. The wealthy relatives to whom she sometimes alluded never came to see her, so that as far as one knew, she was never addressed as Agatha, which name she owned.

Had Miss Billett been a native of the place, there would have been no mystery surrounding her, but she had come as a girl in her teens to a neighbouring village, and taken a situation there in the Manor House. Both her parents had died, and, apart from the mention of her wealthy connections, Miss Billett had given no clear picture of her origin or background.

She remained at the Manor until she retired, then came to live at the cottage where she now resided. It was here that she had gradually accumulated her coterie of helpers, and as the years went by, she became still more a source of envy and conjecture.

There came, however, the day when the mystery began to clear.

At the age of eighty-three Miss Billett became seriously ill, and her helpers flitted continuously to and from her cottage. Then one evening ensued a terrific altercation outside her cottage door. There, assembled at once, were all her six helpers, and a jangling which began in whispers soon became voices raised in anger, and regardless of prying eyes and listening ears their voices broke on the quiet evening air.

"I tell 'ee she asked I t' lay 'er out."

"No, she never, 'twere I. 'Annie,' she said, 'I want fer you t' lay I out an' ivery penny I got shall be yours.' "

"Liars, liars!" several voices shrieked at once. "She asked I." "She asked I."

"For all I done for 'er," said a more subdued and mournful voice "she promised I 'er fortune."

"She promised I." "She promised I." Their voices rose again. "I want fer you t' close me eyes an' lay me out."

"There, bide quiet all o'ee, the poor soul's a-dyin'." This time a hush fell upon them all, and the speaker pushed open the door and went in.

After several days of expectation the little band, so divided on the night of Miss Billett's death, now became united in a common woe. They paused in the street for sad consultations. They lingered after Sunday evening service to whisper and nod and sigh. Scraps of their conversations drifted to those outside their dolorous circle.

"After all I done, the cookin' an' washin' an' cleanin'."

"Ah, 'tis 'ard for 'ee, Maud, I must zay. But you baint the only one."

"Look at I! What about all they puddin's I carried in, an' me 'usband doin' 'er garden year in year out."

"But what about I," another voice said. "I zid 'er breathe 'er last, closed 'er eyes, an' laid 'er out fer burial."

They had gathered around the speaker now, who was regarded as chief mourner for their wrongs.

"Do 'ee know?" she whispered, "thick old woman died wi' a smirk on 'her face, a sneaky kind a' smile."

"An' well she mid, an' well she mid," they chorused grimly and nodded their heads; for Miss Billett had died without a penny to leave.

GHOSTS

THE LAVENDER LADY

The building at Corfe Mullen now called the Lavender Farm was originally known as Corfe Lodge and has been in existence for about 300 years. It is supposed once to have been a shooting-box to which a cottage was added. Later the place became a poultry and cattle farm and the acres around produced large quantities of corn and fattened turkeys and poultry to be sent to London.

About fifty years ago, however, the place became a lavender farm. Instead of the corn, fields of lavender waved in the breeze and double white roses sent their perfume over the village.

The old disused church of St. Andrew nearby, became the "still" and here began the first process in the manufacture of perfume and pot-pourri.

All that remains of the "still" today are the three crumbling pillars which once supported the church of St. Andrew. The barn which housed the corn has been converted to a dwelling. The cottage is inhabited, and the Lodge itself, apart from its present name gives no indication of its past association with the fragrant harvest of the fields.

Nevertheless, until the bombing of the last war damaged the Lodge, a superstition linked the place with its romantic past. Whether it arose from the rather lonely position of the house on the edge of the heath or from imagination applied to unexplained happenings, we cannot, say but there still exists a firm belief that Corfe Lodge is haunted.

The Lodge has changed hands many times since the lavender farm has become disused. No doubt the story of the ghost lost nothing in the telling as the years went by.

The story goes that many years ago a pretty young woman lost her child in the swamp not far from the Lodge and after that time haunted the premises and was seen hurrying across the heath towards the swamp. A pleasing apparition, she wore her hair in two long plaits and was dressed in a crinoline.

I was given details of the ghost from a native of the place who worked on the Lavender Farm at the Corfe Lodge Nurseries. He is convinced that he has seen the apparition many times and vows that once, standing near his little moorland hut, two of his friends saw, as they thought, a young woman approaching. They opened the gate for her, but before reaching it the figure had vanished.

He tells many tales of her appearances.

His sister, he says, who was maid at the Lodge at the time, had many queer manifestations of the Supernatural. Doors opened of their own accord, steps were heard on the landing and once she declared that the ghostly form of the Lavender Lady bent over her bed at night.

Another appearance of the attractive ghost was early one summer morning. Some men had come to work in the fields and saw the figure of a woman which faded before their eyes.

How true is this tale of the Lavender Lady? We have no means of knowing.

My informant is an intelligent man of about 76 years. He has lived in his little hut on the moors for twenty-six years, his companions, Sparkle the dog, five cats, two goats, twelve hens and a magnificent cockerel (fortunately penned).

He is supremely content and declares he would live nowhere else. Billy, as he is known to his many friends, rises at five every morning, cooks his own food on his small kitchen-range, does his own washing and makes his own bed. He goes to work at the nearby Nurseries five days a week.

For lighting, Billy has an oil lamp. He fetches his drinking water from a spring some two hundred yards away on the slope of a hill. He does not smoke. He takes two papers daily and *John Bull* weekly and by means of his little portable radio keeps in touch with the world at large.

Billy's worldly possessions are few but he has a contentment that kings might envy, and a philosophy which a scholar might never achieve.

He enjoys the pure air he breathes on the moors; he fears no man, never worries, is independent even of his own family, yet is friendly withal.

"What would you do if you were taken ill?" asked one of Billy's friends. "I shall never be ill," said Billy.

Seeing the blackened heath from the recent fires so near his hut, "Weren't you afraid?" I enquired. "No," Billy replied, "the grass'll keep the fire from spreadin'."

Billy has no fears, either of the natural or the supernatural. His mind is steeped in memories of the old Lavender Farm, and living in solitude on the moors it is not surprising that his imagination has engendered a belief in the occult.

"If we don't hurry up," Billy is known to have said with relish when darkness began to fall, "We shall see thick 'ooman."

Did the Lavender Lady, as she was called, exist only in Billy's imagination or did the tormented spirit of the young mother really haunt the moors in search of her child who was lost?

We shall never know. Even Billy admits that since the bombing of the last war she has never been seen.